Warwickshire County Council

		JM
NOV 1/19		
6/19 RG		
12/19 RG		
1.4.2020		
12/20 RG		
6/22 RG		
1/23 RG		

KT-449-161

This item is to be returned or renewed before the latest date above. It may be borrowed for a further period if not in demand. **To renew your books:**

- **Phone the 24/7 Renewal Line 01926 499273 or**
- **Visit www.warwickshire.gov.uk/libraries**

Discover ● Imagine● Learn ● *with libraries*

Warwickshire County Council

Working for Warwickshire

Also by Kate Hewitt

Inherited by Ferranti
Moretti's Marriage Command
Demetriou Demands His Child
A Di Sione for the Greek's Pleasure
Engaged for Her Enemy's Heir
The Innocent's One-Night Surrender
Desert Prince's Stolen Bride
Princess's Nine-Month Secret

Seduced by a Sheikh miniseries

The Secret Heir of Alazar
The Forced Bride of Alazar

Discover more at millsandboon.co.uk.

THE SECRET KEPT FROM THE ITALIAN

KATE HEWITT

MILLS & BOON

First Published in Great Britain 2018
by Mills & Boon, an imprint of HarperCollins*Publishers*
1 London Bridge Street, London, SE1 9GF

© 2018 Kate Hewitt

ISBN: 978-0-263-27024-2

MIX
Paper from
responsible sources
FSC® C007454

This book is produced from independently certified FSC™ paper
to ensure responsible forest management.
For more information visit www.harpercollins.co.uk/green.

Printed and bound in Spain
by CPI, Barcelona

CHAPTER ONE

THE THIRTY-SECOND FLOOR of the office building was dark as Maisie Dobson pushed her trolley of cleaning supplies down the hallway, the squeak of the wheels the only sound in the ghostly building. After six months of night cleaning she should be used to the other-worldliness of the experience, but it still freaked her out a little. Although there were half a dozen cleaners in the building, they were all on separate floors, the rooms silent and shadowy, the lights of Manhattan glittering from the floor-to-ceiling windows.

It was two o'clock in the morning and her body ached with fatigue. She had a nine o'clock performance tutorial tomorrow, and she was likely to fall asleep in the middle of it. That had always been her dream—music school, not cleaning. But one meant the other, and that was fine. Maisie was used to working hard for what she wanted.

She paused as a light gleamed from an office down the hallway. Someone had left the light on, she supposed, and yet she couldn't keep a flicker of unease from rippling through her, the little hairs on the nape of her neck prickling. No one had ever left their light on before; most of them were on automatic timers. By the time the team of cleaners arrived at eleven o'clock at night, the high-rise in Manhattan's midtown was completely dark, everyone having gone home. Maisie pushed the trolley onward, the squeak of its wheels sounding even louder in the empty corridor, her heart beginning to thud.

Don't be such a baby, she scolded herself. *There's nothing to be afraid of. It's a light, nothing more.*

She stopped the trolley in front of the lit-up office and then, taking a quick breath, she poked her head around the half-open door… and saw a man.

Maisie stilled, every sense flaring. This wasn't just any man, the usual paunchy corporate stiff staying late. No, this man was… Her mind spun emptily, trying to think of words to describe him. Ink-dark hair flopped over his forehead, and strong, slanted brows were drawn over lowered eyes, so his spiky eyelashes fanned his high, blade-like cheekbones. His mouth was twisted in a grimace as he contemplated the half-empty glass of whisky dangling from his long, lean fingers.

He'd taken off his tie and unbuttoned the top buttons of his shirt, so a sliver of bronzed, muscular chest was visible between the crisp folds of cotton. He fairly pulsated with charismatic, rakish power, so much so that Maisie had taken a step into the room before she even realised what she was doing.

Then he looked up. Piercing blue eyes pinned her to the spot. 'Well, hello,' he drawled, his mouth twisting into a smile that wasn't quite a smile. His voice was low and honeyed, with the trace of an accent. 'How are you this very fine evening?'

Maisie would have felt alarmed or even afraid, except in that moment she saw such anguish in his eyes, in the harsh lines of his face, that her heart twisted inside her and she took another step into the room.

'I'm all right,' she said quietly, taking in the bottle of whisky planted on his desk that was mostly empty. 'I think the real question is, how are you?'

The man tilted his head back, revealing even more of his throat and chest, the glass nearly slipping from his fingers. 'How am I?' he repeated. 'That is a good question. A very good question.'

'Is it?' Maisie said. Something about the man's intense sadness reached in and grabbed hold of her heart. She'd always had a lot of love to give, and so few people to give it to. Her brother, Max, had been the main recipient, but he was independent now, wanting to make his own way. That was a good thing. Of course it was. She just had to keep telling herself that.

'Yes, it is,' the man answered, sitting up and flinging his arms wide so glinting drops of whisky sparkled in the air and then splashed on the floor. 'Because I should be fine, shouldn't I? I should be fantastic.'

Maisie folded her arms. 'Oh? Why should you?' She was intrigued now, as well as empathetic. Who *was* this man? She didn't think he worked here; she'd been cleaning this office building for six months and she'd never seen him. Of course, she hadn't seen many of the men and women who worked here, coming in late as she did, and yet she couldn't escape the sense that this man didn't belong here, in a corner office on a middle floor of an anonymous building. He seemed too different, too powerful, too charismatic. Even drunk, as he had to be, he exuded both charm and strength, making Maisie's stomach fizz in a way it hadn't in a long time, if ever.

She pushed those feelings aside as she waited for his answer, for beyond this man's potent sexual charisma he exuded a pain that reached out to her, inside her, and made her remember her own pain. Her own grief.

'Why should I be fantastic?' The man raised one dark slash of an eyebrow, an amused smile curving his mobile mouth. 'For any number of reasons. I'm wealthy, powerful,

at the top of my career, and I can have any woman I want.'
He laced his fingers together and stretched them over his
head as he stared at the ceiling, a pose that seemed strangely
sad and even vulnerable. 'I have homes in Milan, London
and Crete. I have a forty-foot pleasure yacht, a private jet…'
He lifted his head to laser her with a sardonic, bright blue
gaze. 'Should I go on?'

'No.' Maisie swallowed hard, daunted by that oh-so-
impressive list. This man definitely didn't belong here. He
should be on the top floor with the vice-presidents and
CEO, or have a whole floor to himself. Who on earth *was*
he? 'But I've lived long enough to know those kinds of
things don't make you happy,' she told him, although she
thought they probably helped a little. She couldn't remember a time when money hadn't been tight, the wolf pant-
ing and clawing at the door as she struggled to keep her
and Max afloat.

'You've lived long enough?' Amusement flashed in the
man's eyes, along with a deeper interest. 'You don't look
old enough to have left school.'

'I'm twenty-four,' Maisie answered with dignity. 'And I
am in school. Cleaning offices is my night job.'

'It is night, isn't it?' He turned to stare out of the window, the lights of the Chrysler Building glittering against
a dark and fathomless sky. 'It is a dark, cold, black night.'

His flat voice, the utter bleakness of his tone, sent a ripple of apprehension through Maisie. She was pretty sure
he wasn't talking about the weather.

'Why are you here?' she asked softly. 'Drinking alone
in an empty office building?'

He didn't answer for a long moment, his gaze still on the
dark view outside. Then, like a dog shaking its wet coat,
he turned to her with a sudden smile, bright and hard. 'But
this building isn't empty, and I'm not alone.' He fumbled

for the glass he'd left on the table. 'Why should I drink by myself?' he challenged as he poured a full measure of whisky into the glass and thrust it towards her.

'I can't...' Maisie said, taking a step back as if he'd forced the glass to her lips. 'I'm working.'

He glanced around the room, that amused quirk lifting his lips once more. 'Working?'

'I clean this office building,' Maisie said a bit stiffly. 'This is the last office on the floor.'

'Ah, then you're almost done.'

She was, but it didn't matter. It was nearly three o'clock in the morning and she had school tomorrow. 'I still can't drink,' she said firmly. 'And I really should get on with cleaning...'

He glanced around the room, with its desk, a couple of chairs and a leather sofa against the wall. 'How much can there be to clean?'

'I need to spray all the surfaces, empty the bins, vacuum...' For some unfathomable reason Maisie felt herself blushing as she listed her humble duties.

'Then let me help you,' the man said. 'And then we'll have a drink.'

She stared at him in surprise, his suggestion completely unexpected. 'You don't—'

'I want to.' He sprang up from his chair with surprising alacrity, considering he had to have drunk most of a bottle of whisky, and plucked a spray bottle of cleaning fluid and a cloth from the bucket of supplies Maisie had left by the door. 'Right, here we are.' He swept his papers into a pile and then sprayed the surface of the desk while Maisie watched gormlessly. Nothing like this had ever happened to her before.

Occasionally she'd stumbled across men or women who were pulling a late night at the office, and more often than not they allowed her to work around them while occasionally emitting deep sighs to indicate the inconvenience she was causing. She'd scurry around and then leave as quickly as she could, murmuring an apology.

The man had already finished wiping the desk and was now cleaning the coffee table in front of the sofa. He glanced at her, his eyes full of surprising laughter. 'I'm starting to think you're lazy.'

'Who are you?' Maisie blurted.

'Antonio Rossi.' He finished the table and then reached for the waste-paper basket under the desk and emptied it into the garbage bag hanging from her trolley. 'And who are you?'

'Maisie.'

'Pleased to meet you, Maisie.' He nodded at the vacuum cleaner behind her. 'All that's left to do is a quick vacuum and then we can have that drink.'

She was lovely. Antonio stared at the woman—Maisie, she'd said—in expectation. She looked stunned by his help, and he supposed he was a bit surprised, too. He didn't normally help the cleaning staff, although there was certainly no shame in it. He'd had worse and lower-paid jobs in his lifetime.

But he liked the look of Maisie, with her tumbling auburn curls and wide green eyes, her curvy figure only partially hidden by the shapeless blue coverall she wore as some kind of uniform. He wanted to have a drink with her. He needed to keep forgetting, and over the years he'd found that alcohol was the best way to do that. Sex wasn't far behind.

Slowly, still looking a bit shell-shocked, Maisie turned and reached for the vacuum. She plugged it in and then, impatient, Antonio reached for the handle. Her head jerked up in surprise, curls bouncing around her heart-shaped face. Freckles were scattered across her nose like gold dust.

'I'll do it,' he said, and he whipped around with the vacuum, the noise filling the space and vibrating in his chest, only for the silence they were plunged into when he cut the power to feel expectant and hushed.

Slowly Antonio wrapped the cord around the handle while Maisie simply stared. He wasn't so drunk that he didn't feel a flicker of guilty unease at seducing a cleaner in an empty office building in the middle of the night. But then, she would either be a willing partner or she would walk away; was there really anything to atone for here? He already had enough sins to deal with.

Besides, it might not even go that way. Maybe she was married, or had a serious boyfriend. Except he didn't think he was imagining the spark that had snapped to life between them when their eyes had met. Just to test it, he brushed her fingers with his as he put the vacuum away, and he felt a leap inside him as he saw her pupils flare. Yes, it was there. It was definitely there.

'So,' he said. 'Shall we have that drink?'

'I really shouldn't…'

Already her willpower was starting to crumble. Antonio fished another tumbler from the desk drawer and poured a generous measure.

'Shouldn't is such a dull word, don't you think? We shouldn't let our lives be ruled by shouldn'ts.'

'Isn't that an oxymoron?'

He laughed, impressed by her quick wit. 'Exactly,' he said, and handed her a glass. She took it, her pale, slender fingers wrapping around it as she studied him.

'Why are you here?'

'I suppose it depends what you mean by here.' He took a sip of whisky, willing her to taste her own. The burn of alcohol at the back of his throat and the ensuing fire in his belly were a welcome comfort.

'In this empty office building, late at night, drinking by yourself.'

'I was working.' At least he had been, until the dark memories had started crowding in, taking him over, as they did on this day every year. And so many other days, as well, if he let them.

'Do you work here?' She sounded disbelieving.

'Not as such. I've been hired for a certain job.'

'What's that?'

He hesitated, because, while the takeover was common knowledge, he didn't want to encourage gossip. But then he decided she was harmless, and she probably didn't know anyone who worked here anyway.

'I assess the risks involved in a corporate takeover,' he said. 'And try to minimise loss and damage during the hand-over of power.'

Her eyes widened. 'This company's being taken over?'

'Yes.' He cocked his head, noting her look of alarm. 'Do you know anyone who works here?'

'Only the other cleaners. Will…will our jobs be at risk?'

'I shouldn't think so. Offices will always need to be cleaned.'

'Oh.' Her tense shoulders slumped a little in relief. 'Good.'

'Shall we toast to that?' Antonio suggested lightly. 'Yours are some of the only jobs that won't be affected.'

'Oh.' Her mouth, lush and pink, turned down at the corners. 'That's sad.'

'But not for you.'

'No…'

He raised his glass. *'Cincin.'*

Slowly, so slowly, she took a sip of whisky, wrinkling

her nose at the taste of the alcohol, but swallowing it without a splutter.

'What does *cincin* mean?'

'It's a common toast in Italy.'

'Ah.' She nodded. 'Is that where you're from?'

'Guilty.' The word sprang to his lips and soured his gut. *Guilty.* He was so guilty, and not simply for his heritage. For so much more. Things he could never undo. Things he could never forget, even if he tried to let himself.

'I've never been to Italy.' She sounded wistful. 'Is it beautiful?'

'Parts are very beautiful.'

Maisie looked down, and then took another sip of whisky, shuddering a little as the liquor went down. 'It tastes like fire.'

'Feels like it, too.' Antonio tossed back the last of his drink, savouring the burn, craving the oblivion. If he closed his eyes he'd see his brother's face, the smile curving his mouth, his eyes sparkling, everything in him young and carefree for a moment. If he kept his eyes closed that face would change, turn lifeless and pale, the pavement beneath his head wine-red with blood even though he'd never seen his brother like that. Never had the chance.

That was why he needed to keep drinking. So he could close his eyes

'Why are you here?' Maisie asked softly. She'd lowered her glass and was giving him a searching look, her eyes wide and so very green. 'I don't mean work. I mean drinking alone late at night.' Antonio shrugged, about to say something dismissive about needing to work late, but then she skewered him with her next sorrowful observation. 'You looked so sad. As sad as I've felt.'

The quiet admission pierced him right through. 'You've felt…?'

Her lips twisted, her lashes sweeping down to hide her gaze. 'My parents died when I was nineteen. When I looked at you, that's what I thought about. You looked…you looked the way I felt then. Sometimes the way I still feel.'

Her honesty felled him. He'd never encountered such raw, simple truth, unvarnished, unafraid. It humbled him and it left him speechless. Finally he found some words, but they weren't the ones he'd expected. 'That's because I've lost someone as well, and I was thinking about him tonight.'

What? He never talked about Paolo. Not to anyone. Certainly not to a stranger. He tried not to think about him, but of course he always did. Paolo was always on the fringes of his mind, in the corners of his soul. Haunting him. Accusing him. Making him remember.

'Who did you lose?' Her eyes were sad and yet full of compassion, her face so heartbreakingly lovely. Her auburn hair framed her face in a curly, fiery nimbus, and her mouth was lush, her expression open. Antonio wanted to sweep her into his arms, but more than that he wanted to talk to her. He wanted to tell her the truth, or at least as much of the truth as he could bear to reveal.

'My brother,' he said quietly. 'My little brother.'

CHAPTER TWO

'Oh.' The word was a soft gasp as Maisie looked at this man, this beautiful man, who was so obviously still grieving. Her heart ached for him. 'I'm so sorry.'

He jerked one powerful shoulder in a shrug. 'Thank you.'

'I have a little brother. I can't imagine...' She couldn't bear to lose Max. Not after everything else. He was all she had, and now that he'd finished university he was living his own life, claiming an independence that made her feel both proud and sad. It was finally time to chase her own dreams, but sometimes that was a lonely occupation.

'Yet you lost your parents.' Antonio shoved his hands in his pockets and strolled towards the window, his shuttered gaze on the city skyline. 'How did that happen?'

'A car accident.'

His shoulders tensed and he stilled. 'A drunk driver?'

'No, just someone going too fast. Ran a red light and ploughed head-on into their car.' She took a quick, steadying breath. Five years later it still hurt. It was no longer the fresh, stinging, open wound, but more the ache of an old but deep injury that would always be a part of her. 'The mercy was they both died instantly.'

He let out a huff of utterly humourless laughter. 'Some mercy.'

'It's something,' Maisie said quietly. Sometimes it had felt like all she had. 'How did your younger brother die?'

Antonio didn't answer for a moment; Maisie felt instinctively he was wondering how much to say. Debating how much to tell her. 'The same,' he finally answered tonelessly. 'A car accident.' He paused. 'Just like your parents.'

'I'm sorry.' He nodded in acknowledgement, his jaw tight. 'It's hard, sometimes, to think someone's recklessness caused the death of someone you love, isn't it?'

'Yes,' Antonio said, his voice flat. 'Very hard.'

'Was it someone going too fast, or—?'

'Yes.' He cut her off, his voice terse and flat. 'Someone was going too fast.'

Belatedly Maisie realised he might not want to rake over such details. 'I'm sorry,' she said, and impulsively she crossed to him and laid one hand on his arm. He'd rolled up his shirtsleeves and her fingers curled over his bare forearm, the skin warm and taut beneath her palm. An arrow of sensation pierced her core, surprising her with its intensity. She nearly snatched her hand away, and yet for some reason she didn't. Couldn't.

They remained that way, both frozen, for a few taut seconds and then Antonio slowly turned. Maisie saw the heat in his piercing blue eyes, and she felt it in herself, a flood of warmth and need that doused all rational thought. She stared at him, knowing she couldn't hide her expression, her desire. She'd been wanting only to comfort him; at least she thought she had, but now she felt something else entirely. Something overwhelming.

She drew a breath and it hitched audibly. Antonio's eyes flared again. Maisie stared at him, feeling trapped, but in a wonderful way. An exciting way.

'How old is your younger brother?' Antonio asked quietly, and the exquisite tension didn't break, but it lessened.

Maisie took another careful breath and removed her hand from his arm; already she missed the warmth of his skin.

'He's twenty-two now.'

'So he was seventeen when your parents died.'

Surprise and a strange kind of gratification rippled through her at his swift recall. 'Yes.'

'What did you do? Without your parents?'

'Worked.' She didn't want to get into the whole tedious sob story of her parents' sudden death, the ensuing shock that they had no savings and her family home had been double-mortgaged. Money had always been a concern in Maisie's childhood, but she hadn't realised what an overwhelming fear it could be until after her parents' death. But surely a man like Antonio Rossi, with his yacht and his houses and his glittering career, didn't want to hear about that.

'Worked,' Antonio repeated slowly, his gaze searching her face. 'Did you take care of your brother?'

'Yes.' Maisie couldn't keep the ferocity from her tone. Max had been everything to her after her parents had died. She was still finding it hard not to have him at the centre of her world. Even with her new life in the city, she missed him. She missed him needing her, but of course he hadn't needed her for a while. Not emotionally, anyway.

'What's his name?' Antonio asked softly, and for some reason his interest nearly undid her.

'Max,' she whispered. 'He just finished university in the spring. He's doing an internship on Wall Street.'

'Wall Street.' Antonio gave a low whistle. 'Sounds like you've done a good job.'

'I tried.' Maisie dragged her gaze away from Antonio's eyes with effort. 'But we were talking about you.'

'Were we?'

'What was your brother's name?'

Antonio hesitated, and Maisie realised it was an intimate, even invasive question. She understood instinctively that he didn't talk about his brother; that already she was privileged to know as much, or really as little, as she did. 'Paolo,' he finally said, and the word escaped from him on a reluctant sigh. 'He was five years younger than me. He died ten years ago today.'

'Today…'

'Hence the whisky.' He let out a humourless laugh. 'I always find January sixteenth one of the hardest days of the year.'

'I'm so sorry.'

He shrugged, his gaze sliding away from hers. 'It's not your fault.'

'I know that.' She smiled sadly, wanting to touch him again, to offer him that basic comfort, and yet afraid of his response—and hers. 'But I also know how much it hurts. And I'm sorry that you're hurting in that way. I wouldn't wish it on anyone.'

'No.' He glanced back at her, his gaze heavy-lidded now, turning sensual. 'You are a very kind person, Maisie. You have a generous heart, to give so much to people and probably receive less in return.'

She laughed uncertainly. 'That makes me sound a little bit like a doormat,' she observed.

'Not at all.' He cocked his head. 'Is that how you feel?'

Surprise flared through her at his perception, because the truth was she'd always felt, in the darkest corner of her heart, that she gave more to Max, loved him more, than he did her. But that was the nature of their relationship, wasn't it? There were only two years between them but she'd become both mother and father to him. She'd had to. And she'd wanted to, but…sometimes her life had felt dreary, thankless. Sometimes she'd wondered if there was anything more, even as she missed his active presence in her life now. 'Maybe a little,' she admitted, and then felt wretched. How could she begrudge her brother anything, never mind her own love? 'Not really...'

'Shh.' Antonio pressed his finger to her lips, utterly silencing her. 'You don't have to apologise for your feelings. It's already obvious to me how much you care about your brother, and how much you've sacrificed for him.'

'How could you possibly know that?' Maisie whispered, her lips brushing his fingers with every syllable. He kept his finger there, pressed to her lips, light as a feather and yet feeling like the most intimate thing she'd ever experienced.

His gaze was dark and hooded as he replied, 'Because it shines from you. Love and...and goodness.'

From someone else it would have sounded like sentimental flattery, but Antonio's tone was so gentle and sincere, with a touch of sorrow that made Maisie ache. No one had ever said such things to her before. No one had ever even noticed all she'd done for Max. All she'd given up for herself. And somehow this beautiful stranger had.

'Thank you,' she whispered, and Antonio pressed his finger more firmly against her mouth, a caress that Maisie felt to her core. She shuddered, unable to stop herself, and Antonio smiled.

'So loving,' he murmured as he traced the outline of her lips with his fingertip. 'And so lovely.'

Maisie remained transfixed under his touch; the touch of his fingers felt as if he were imprinting himself on her soul. She'd had a few boyfriends over the years, but none of them had been serious—there had been Max to think of, and life was so busy, working full-time and trying to keep up with her music. Those boyfriends' kisses and clinches hadn't affected her the way Antonio Rossi did, by simply touching her lips with the tip of his finger. Not remotely.

Some hazy part of her brain was telling her that she needed to stop this nonsense and get back to work. Finish her shift and go home and forget the dangerous magic that was being wrought in this room, making her insides fizz and the air shimmer.

Antonio trailed his finger from her lips to her chin and then down to the hollow in her throat, where her pulse beat frantically. He rested it there, his brows drawn together as he studied her. He glanced at her from underneath heavy-lidded eyes and then he dropped his finger lower, undoing her coverall and skimming under the plain white T-shirt she wore beneath, with the cleaning company's insignia on the breast pocket.

Shock and desire crashed through Maisie in a double wave and the half-full tumbler of whisky dropped from her nerveless fingers and fell onto the floor, the alcohol soaking into the carpet and filling the air with its pungent scent.

She gasped and looked down in horror. 'Oh, no...'

'It doesn't matter...'

'It does. I can't leave a mess in an office I've just cleaned.'

'Then we won't leave it.'

He smiled, the wry yet intent look in his eyes as good as telling her that this was not going to serve as a distraction from his true purpose, or at least not for long. Yet what did he, magnetic sexy billionaire that he was, want with her?

Of course, the answer was glaringly obvious. Maisie blinked, rooted to the spot, as Antonio fetched a cloth and some carpet cleaner and began to scrub the stain.

He wanted sex. That was what rich, powerful men wanted with women like her. The only thing. Yet here he was, cleaning the carpet for her. She didn't understand him. She didn't understand herself, and how she could actually be tempted by such a sordid proposition.

Sex with a stranger. That was what she was actually thinking about right now. Yet perhaps Antonio wasn't thinking of sex at all; perhaps he was just being kind, a little flirty, humouring the housekeeper. Pure mortification shot through her, turning her insides to ice and her face fiery. Hot and cold, that was how she felt. Hot and cold right through.

Antonio tossed the cleaning supplies back onto her trolley and then straightened, turning to her with a wickedly sexy smile.

'Now, then,' he said. 'Where were we?'

She was blushing, right to the roots of her hair. Antonio noted her change in colour with interest, just as he'd noted the way she'd responded to his finger against her lips. And he'd responded, desire arrowing through him along with something deeper. He'd meant what he said when he'd told her she was loving and good. She seemed, at that moment, like the most uncomplicated, honest and kind person he'd ever encountered, and he craved that as much as he craved her body. Well, almost.

Maisie tilted her chin a little, her eyes flashing emerald fire. 'Where were we, exactly?' she asked, her voice a little croaky yet full of challenge and bravado.

Antonio smiled. 'I think,' he murmured as he skimmed his fingers along her cheek, her skin like warm satin under their tips, 'we were right here.'

Maisie closed her eyes, gritting her teeth as if she had to endure his touch and yet Antonio knew better. Her whole body trembled as if she was strung through with a wire and he was plucking it. 'Why are you doing this to me?' she whispered.

'I haven't even kissed you yet.'

She opened her eyes, shocked despite everything that had already happened, the tension crackling in the air. 'Yet?'

'Yet,' Antonio confirmed. 'Surely, Maisie, you know it's only a matter of time? You want me and I want you. Very much. I want to forget all the grief and sadness, and I want to remember...this.' Gently, so she could pull away if she really wanted to, he drew her towards him. Their hips bumped and her breasts brushed his chest. Her body quivered and her eyes looked like huge, glassy pools, the colour of ferns.

Part of him, a large part, wanted to drive his hands through her wild, auburn hair and plunder her mouth, lose himself in the oblivion of lust with no thought to the wide-eyed woman before him.

But of course he couldn't do that. Maisie was too lovely for such coarse treatment. So he took his time, letting his gaze move slowly over her as she adjusted to being so near to him, the shift in their bodies as well as the shift in the air. Flirtation had turned to anticipation. Expectation.

'You're very lovely,' he murmured as he wound a reddish curl around his finger, tugging it gently so she had to come even closer. 'Very, very lovely.'

'So are you,' she returned on a shaky laugh. 'But you must know how handsome you are.'

He laughed, because there was something so delightfully refreshing about her artless candour. 'Maybe you could show me.'

She sucked in a breath and then shook her head. 'I wouldn't know how.'

He tugged that curl again. 'You could kiss me.'

A lovely pink blush washed over her face in a tide of colour. 'I...couldn't.'

'You could.'

'I wouldn't know how,' she repeated, her face even fierier now.

'So I'm meant to do all the work and seduce you?' he teased gently, and she bit her lip.

'You don't have to,' she muttered, looking away. 'It's not like I'm asking.'

He laughed softly, enjoying the repartee as much as the delicious anticipation of her kiss. 'I'm asking,' he told her. 'In fact, I'm demanding.'

'Demanding...?'

'Kiss me, Maisie.'

She turned back to him with wide, shocked eyes. He would have thought she was offended except for the flare of excitement in their emerald-bright depths, the way her teeth sank into her lower lip as she considered his request—no, his demand.

'You're looking at my mouth like it's a mountain to climb,' he observed wryly. They'd barely touched and he was finding it hard to hold on to his light, laughing manner. The need was growing inside him—a torrent, a torment, and soon it would be overwhelming.

'It feels like it,' Maisie admitted. 'I'm not... I'm not adventurous.'

'But you want to kiss me.' It was a statement, not a question. He saw and felt her answer in the tremble of her body, the dilation of her pupils, the way her tongue darted out to moisten her plump pink lips.

'Yes...'

Antonio drew back a little. 'You sound uncertain.' But only a little.

'This is so outside my realm of experience,' Maisie said on a huff of disbelieving laughter. 'I feel like I've fallen into a fairy tale or down a rabbit hole.'

'Then enjoy the ride,' Antonio suggested. He wondered

briefly about warning her that this was a one-night stand, a brief moment of pleasure. But he didn't want to break the mood and surely it was obvious? Relationships didn't start between strangers on an empty office floor at two o'clock in the morning. Maisie seemed refreshingly honest and artless, but she wasn't dumb.

'Enjoy the ride,' she repeated slowly, savouring each word as if it were a sip of fine wine. 'Now, that's something I don't think I've ever done before.'

Antonio raised his eyebrows. 'No?'

'No. Definitely not.'

'Then maybe now is the time.'

Maisie took a deep, slow breath and raised her resolute gaze to his. Antonio felt a blaze of triumph burn through him; he knew that look. She'd made up her mind.

'Maybe I should,' she said, and then she stood on her tiptoes and brushed her lips against his, feather-light, whisper-soft. Antonio remained still under her hesitant caress, waiting to see what she would do next. She drew back, frowning a little. 'Didn't you…didn't you like it?'

'Of course I liked it,' Antonio was quick to reassure her. 'But how can I be satisfied with barely a mouthful when what I really want is a meal? A feast?' He let her see the heat simmering in his gaze as his mouth dropped to her lips. This really was the most interesting and exquisite foreplay, and like nothing else he'd ever done with a woman. 'Kiss me again, Maisie.'

And she did, this time pressing her body as well as her lips against his, one slender hand curling over his shoulder. It was clumsy and hesitant and somehow perfect. This time Antonio couldn't keep from responding. He spanned her waist with his hands, revelling in her softness, and drew her even more snugly against him, so their bodies were in sensual alignment. He felt a shudder go through her at his obvious arousal, and he paused, waiting for her to catch up. To take the next step.

And she did, kissing him again, her tongue darting out to touch his lips like a shy butterfly. Antonio captured her mouth against his own, deepening the kiss, plundering her silken depths as he'd been longing to.

Need roared through him, his blood rushing through his veins, pounding in his head. He'd meant to go slowly, to be civilised and controlled about the whole thing, but all his careful plans fell apart as Maisie gave herself to him so generously, so artlessly. He backed her up across the room, all the way to the sofa, and his last remnant of self-control kept him from practically throwing her onto its leather cushions. Instead he laid her down gently, and she stared up at him with wide, shocked eyes.

'Antonio…'

His breath came out in a ragged hiss as he stared down at her, aghast at the possibility of her having second thoughts. 'Do you want me, Maisie?'

'Yes…' Her voice wavered and Antonio cursed himself for having rushed things.

'Do you want this?' He gestured to the space between them, the look in his eyes surely leaving no confusion as to what he meant.

Maisie lay on the sofa, her pupils dilated, her lips slightly parted, her expression dazed and full of desire. She drew in a long, slow breath, her gaze searching him, asking silent questions Antonio didn't know how to answer. He waited, fists clenched, everything taut and expectant, as he braced himself for her reply.

'Yes,' she whispered finally, and her head fell back against the cushions. 'Yes, I do.'

CHAPTER THREE

MAISIE GAZED UP at Antonio's intent and beautiful face and felt a peaceful settling inside her; a resolution had been made. She was going to do this. She was going to sleep with him. She wasn't sure when she had decided. When she'd kissed him? When he'd told her he wanted her? When she'd come into the room?

She didn't do stuff like this. Of course she didn't. For the last five years her entire focus had been on Max—caring for him, providing for him, and suppressing all her hopes, dreams and needs. And maybe that was why she had decided, why she was lying on a sofa looking up at the most beautiful man she'd ever seen, waiting for him to start seducing her. Because she'd lived for someone else for too long, and now, just for one night, she wanted to live for herself. For pleasure. For excitement. For this.

Antonio's gaze roved over her. 'You're sure,' he said slowly.

'Yes.' She swallowed, more of a gulp. 'Yes, I'm sure.'

'Good,' he answered swiftly. 'Because so am I.'

Her heart trembled as he knelt before her, his hands on her hips, anchoring her in place. She stared at him, feeling as pinned—and as beautiful—as a butterfly. Waiting.

Then he lowered his mouth to hers and her mind blissfully emptied out. This was what had happened the first time he'd kissed her, or rather, she'd kissed him. Barely a brush of lips and yet her senses, every single one, had short-circuited. She hadn't been able to think. She had barely remembered to breathe. The touch of his mouth to hers had felt like a spark to her soul, lighting a fire within her. And when Antonio had taken control of their kiss it had become a complete conflagration. She was *consumed.*

And Maisie felt consumed now, in the best possible way, as his mouth moved over hers—and then lower. He kissed his way down her cheek and throat, his tongue touching the hard edge of her collarbone before nestling in the hollow of her throat, sucking and teasing. A shudder escaped her and she arched up, already helpless.

Antonio chuckled against her skin and then his mouth moved lower, to the edge of her blue T-shirt. 'What are you wearing?' he murmured and Maisie squirmed and blushed.

'My cleaning uniform. It's hideous, I know...'

'Clearly you could inflame me wearing a bin bag,' Antonio returned as his hands slid under the shapeless shirt. 'But I think I'd like to see you wearing nothing at all.'

He slid her T-shirt over her head and tossed it across the room with a deliberately wolfish smile that would have made Maisie laugh if she didn't feel so suddenly, unbearably exposed. She struggled not to cover herself; no one had seen her in just her bra. *No one.*

'You are even lovelier than before,' Antonio said softly. 'There's no need to be embarrassed.'

Maisie swallowed, not quite willing to admit that no one had ever seen her like this before. That Antonio Rossi, a virtual stranger, was the first. With his gaze steady he reached one hand out and cupped her breast, his palm warm through the thin cotton of her bra. Sparks of sensation radiated outward from his touch, fireworks fizzing inside her. Although she tried to hide her reaction, Antonio noticed and smiled.

'Do you know how potent a woman's reaction is to a man? How inflaming?'

'But you're still dressed,' Maisie protested. She wanted him to touch her more; she wanted to touch him. She just had no idea how to go about it.

'That is something that can be easily remedied.' He lifted his hands to the buttons of his shirt and then paused, one eyebrow arched. 'Perhaps you will do it for me?'

'Oh…' She hadn't expected a man like Antonio—powerful, privileged, and surely used to being in charge—to give her so much control. Want her to have it. 'I…'

He shrugged, his expression one of wry amusement although there was a fierce light in his eyes. 'They're just buttons.'

Yes, they were just buttons, of course they were, and yet it was so much more. It was owning the reckless choice she'd made, and taking control of it. It was being bolder and more daring and more sexual than she'd ever been in her life.

Slowly Maisie raised herself up on one elbow and then, with fingers that trembled only a little, she started undoing the buttons of his crisp white shirt. Every time she inhaled she breathed in the clean, woodsy scent of his aftershave; every time she managed to slip a button through its hole she glimpsed a tantalising bit of his chest, bronzed skin over sculpted muscle.

Antonio's breath came out in a hiss between his teeth, and with a jolt Maisie realised how affected he was. How *she* affected him. He must have seen her surprised expression, for he laughed softly and said, 'I've told you how you make me feel, haven't I? Now you can see the proof for yourself.' The buttons undone, he reached for her hand and laid it flat against his bare chest, over the thudding of his heart, its hectic pace matching her own.

They remained that way for a long, suspended moment, connected by her hand on his heart, all of it feeling so wonderfully and excruciatingly intense. This was so *intimate,* and not simply because she no longer had a shirt on. She hadn't expected it somehow, along with the physical pleasure, the overwhelming need. She felt an emotional connection with this man that had begun when she'd seen him looking so sad, and its natural continuation was here.

Maisie spread her fingers against his chest, revelling in the taut muscle, the satiny skin. Another breathless moment passed, and then she looked up at him, waiting, wanting—and everything changed.

It was as if a spark had suddenly caught the tinder, seeming to take them both by surprise. Antonio pulled her towards him, crushing her breasts against his chest as his mouth came down on hers, hard and demanding. And Maisie answered that demand, wrapping her arms around his neck, driving her fingers through his hair as she offered herself to him utterly.

She fell back against the sofa, Antonio's body pressing into hers, one powerful thigh sliding between her legs, creating an even deeper urgency.

He tore his mouth from hers and moved it lower, a shuddering gasp escaping her as her eyes fluttered closed and his lips nudged aside the thin cotton of her bra.

Her body arced off the sofa as he continued his soft and deft exploration, unclasping her bra so swiftly Maisie barely realised it had gone, and she was naked from the waist up. Her mind was blurred with sensation, fiery arrows of pleasure shooting through her as Antonio continued to explore her body with his lips and hands.

Her baggy trousers followed her shirt and bra, and then her underwear as well, so without even fully realising it was happening she was naked, and so was Antonio. She gazed up at him, his skin burnished in the dim light from the desk lamp, his chest taut and muscled and perfect.

Maisie trembled against the sofa, aware, even in her pleasure-dazed state, what a step she was taking. Enormous. Irrevocable.

Antonio must have sensed something of her feelings, for he paused, his hands braced on either side of her head, his breathing harsh and ragged.

'Maisie…you are sure?' She nodded, too overwhelmed to speak. 'Tell me,' he urged. 'Tell me to go on, or tell me to stop.'

She drew a deep breath into her lungs, her body splayed and open to his. 'Yes,' she whispered, and reached up to lace her fingers around his neck, bringing his mouth down to hers. 'I'm sure.'

Antonio needed no more encouragement. He kissed her hard on the mouth as his hips pressed against hers, and Maisie stiffened at the sudden and strange invasion of her body. He frowned slightly, and she wondered if he knew she'd never done this before. Did her inexperience show?

Antonio let out a groan as he slid fully inside her, and Maisie tried not to flinch, adjusting to the feeling of him. So this was sex. She thought she liked the foreplay a bit better.

Antonio lifted his head, his frown deepening as he looked at her. 'Maisie…'

'It's all right.' It suddenly felt important that he should not know she was—or had been—a virgin. That she'd chosen to give her virginity to a stranger she'd never see again. She arched up, drawing him more fully into her body, wrapping her legs around his hips.

Antonio began to move with slow, deliberate thrusts, and as she adjusted to the feel of him a flicker of pleasure began to grow. Maisie started to match his rhythm, and the flicker grew into flame, their bodies moving in union as the fire began to rage.

She lost all sense of time or place or comportment, both of them searching and straining for the height of the pleasure, until it burst like an explosion of flame, Maisie's jagged cry renting the air before she fell back against the sofa, emotionally and physically spent.

Antonio rested his forehead against Maisie's for a brief moment as he fought to hold on to his composure, half amazed that it was proving to be such a painful challenge.

Sex on an office sofa with a woman whose last name he didn't know wasn't a completely new experience. But this—with Maisie—felt different. It felt overwhelming.

He hadn't expected the emotion. He didn't *do* emotion, except on the anniversary of his brother's death, and then he indulged in it only by himself, giving in to the grief he locked away all year in a single, torturous night. He never should have invited Maisie in on this night of all nights, never should have seduced her when he'd felt so raw and emotionally exposed.

He never should have cracked open the door to his tightly guarded heart, even just a sliver. But now he had and he couldn't keep the flood of grief and sorrow from rushing through that sliver and drowning him.

He rolled onto his side, pulling Maisie with him, and buried his head in the warm, soft curve of her neck. He was still trying to hold on to his composure, even though he knew it was a lost cause; he'd given it up when he'd buried himself in her body, when she'd put her arms around him and drawn him in even deeper, and he'd felt whole and lost at the same time.

Now shudders racked his body and his arms tightened around her, holding on to her as if she was his anchor. And she did anchor him, wrapping her arms around him, her fingers stroking his hair, whispering words of endearment and comfort as if he were a child.

It was so weak, so shaming, and yet so necessary. He couldn't hold it together any more. He just couldn't. And he hated that even as he burrowed against her, seeking the comfort only she could provide.

'You loved him very much,' Maisie said softly, after a few moments when the only sound had been Antonio's ragged breathing.

'Yes.' He practically gasped the word out, his eyes shut. 'Yes, I did. And...' Somehow he felt compelled to speak, to let her know the awful, unvarnished truth, or at least some of it. 'It was my fault he died.'

Her hands stilled on his hair and he held his breath, waiting for her verdict. Her condemnation. 'Did you kill him?' she asked quietly, and he nearly jerked back in shock at the bold, bald question.

'No! Not like that—'

'Then it wasn't your fault.'

His breath came out in a low, defeated rush. If only it were so easy. He'd accept her absolution and walk away a free man. But Antonio knew better than that, and if he told Maisie the full truth, so would she. 'You can't say that.'

'And you can't say you killed him.' Her soft hand slid down to frame his face and she tilted his chin up so he was forced to look at her. Her eyes, sparkling with tears, were the colour of moss as she held his face in her hands and spoke words of tenderness. 'That's why you looked so sad tonight,' she said softly, more a statement than a question. 'Because you are bearing the guilt of his death, and no one can carry that kind of weight.'

'You don't know—'

'Then tell me.'

He shook his head, unwilling even now. Especially now. She would hate him then, especially considering her own loss. As little as they had shared, he wanted—needed—to preserve it. Preserve the memory of this night, for it would sustain him for a long time to come.

'Oh, Antonio.' She brushed a kiss across his lips and he closed his eyes, receiving it as the balm he knew it was. 'Grieving is hard enough without adding blame.'

'You don't know,' he said again. It was all he had to offer.

'I know enough,' Maisie told him, her lips a breath away from his. 'I feel enough. I see enough in your eyes.' She kissed him again, and then she kissed both of his closed eyes, and Antonio lay there, aching and open, accepting her caresses even though each one broke something inside him. Chipped another piece off his ossified heart, until at some point there would be nothing left.

Her hair fanned across his chest as she continued to kiss him, her mouth moving lower, her lips pressing softly against his chest, as if she was learning every inch of his body. Amidst the ache of sorrow and grief, he felt desire stir, not the insistent, urgent thing it had been moments ago, but something far deeper and more tender, something more alarming and far more wonderful. He knew he couldn't resist.

She rolled on top of him, her hair like a fiery blanket covering them both. Antonio slid his hands down to her hips, both anchoring and guiding her. Her breath hitched and he knew she felt it too, not just the desire but the depth of emotion. They'd shared so much more than their bodies tonight. They'd given each other glimpses of their souls.

They came together slowly this time, naturally, with her straddling his hips, her hands braced on his shoulders as she enveloped him in her body. The sense of completion and rightness nearly took his breath away. He'd had plenty of sexual encounters in his lifetime, but he'd never felt anything like this. Everything had ratcheted up to an exquisite degree, the intensity and the emotion and the pleasure.

Antonio gazed up at her as they moved together in sensuous rhythm, and she looked back, her eyes full of compassion and sorrow as well as desire. As they climbed towards that dizzying peak of sensation together he felt as if she were part of him, as if she'd imbued herself right into his skin, his soul. He clung to her, and she clung back, acting as one as they went over the precipice.

Afterwards she curled into him, her palm resting over his thudding heart, and he wrapped a tendril of her hair around his wrist, as if he could anchor her there. Their breath came in ragged draws and tears; neither of them spoke, but then they didn't need to speak. Words were superfluous to the purest form of communication they'd just shared.

They must have dozed briefly, for Antonio woke suddenly to a cramp in his neck and a noise in the hall. The room felt cold, the sweat dried on his skin. Maisie was still sleeping next to him.

He lay there, trying to process everything, but the peace and pleasure that had flooded him earlier were replaced by a cold, creeping trickle of horror—and shame. What on earth had he been thinking? What had he *done*?

He remembered the way he'd shuddered in her arms, the words he'd choked out, the weakness and need he'd shown, and everything in him cringed. He'd spent his entire life, and especially the last ten years, keeping himself distant, cutting off his emotions and certainly his heart from anyone and everyone. It was better that way, safer for him, safer for others. And in the space of one evening, no more than an hour, Maisie had cracked him open like an egg.

He felt horribly exposed, as if she'd peeled back his skin,

so that every tender nerve was laid open and stinging. He couldn't stand it, and he couldn't account for it, either. Why had she reached him when no one else had?

It must have been the whisky—what else could it have been? He'd been drunk and sentimental and he'd taken liberties with his own emotions, never mind Maisie's, in the most appalling fashion. All he could do now was claw back what he could.

She stirred next to him and he froze, his eyes clenched shut because he couldn't stand the thought of looking into her face and seeing pity.

Another sound from the hall, and now that he was fully awake he recognised the squeak of a cleaning trolley. 'Maisie?' a woman called.

Maisie stirred again, and then raised her head.

'Maisie, are you here? Are you finished on this floor?'

'Oh, no.' The words came out as a gasp as Maisie rose on one elbow. She glanced at Antonio; he felt it like a scorching mark even though he didn't open his eyes. It might have been the cowardly thing to do, but as she disentangled herself from him and began hopping around the room, scrambling for her clothes, he pretended he was asleep.

'Maisie—'

'I'm here,' she called back, her voice soft and urgent. 'Just—just wait.'

Antonio heard the snick and slither of her clothes as she dressed herself. He cracked open an eye and saw her pulling her hair into a ponytail, her movements quick. She glanced back at him, and through his barely open lids he saw a look of indecision flit across her face, quickly followed by sorrow. She scooped up her pail of cleaning supplies and then the door clicked softly shut behind her.

Antonio breathed out a sigh of relief. It was better this way. It had to be.

CHAPTER FOUR

MAISIE SPENT THE next two weeks in a virtual stupor of shock. She couldn't believe what she'd done, how she'd acted with Antonio Rossi. It had been some form of madness, almost as if she'd taken some drug that had swept away all her inhibitions, taken all her common sense. What had she been *thinking*?

Yet beyond that, she couldn't keep from reliving the tender moments she'd shared with him, an intimacy far beyond anything she'd ever known or even imagined. When he'd cried in her arms…when she'd held him…when she'd taken him inside her body…

Even now, many days later, Maisie felt an ache of longing, a welter of regret and wistfulness. She'd even wondered if he would try to get in touch with her; surely it wouldn't be difficult for a man as powerful as him to find out who she was or where she lived.

In the next moment she berated herself for such schoolgirl stupidity. Of course he wasn't going to get in touch with her. It had been a one-night stand; she wasn't so naïve that she didn't realise that. And yet. And yet. She hadn't been the only one blown away by the intensity of the experience. She felt that deeply, had seen the same sense of wonder in his face that she'd felt inside. The intense level of intimacy had been mutual, she was sure of it.

What if she hadn't scuttled away, scared that she'd be discovered by another one of the cleaners, and perhaps even fired? What if she'd stayed, and they'd talked? What if their one-night stand had bloomed into something greater, and he'd stayed in New York, seen her again...?

It was the stuff of fairy tales and romcoms, and Maisie tried not to think about it too much. She knew how life really worked. It was hard and unfair and didn't turn out the way you expected or wanted. Yes, there was happiness and love, but you had to fight for them both. Fight hard. They didn't fall into your lap in the middle of the night in an empty office block.

She needed to chalk it up as an experience, one that was good, bad, phenomenal, life-changing, heartbreaking. And over.

Maisie tried to focus on her studies, which was usually the thing that brought her the most joy. After deferring her entrance to Juilliard by five years, she was finally doing what she most wanted in life. But even as she went to her performance tutorials and studied music theory, even as she accompanied some friends to a concert in a local church, she felt a little lost, a bit empty. It wasn't a good feeling, and Maisie was annoyed with herself for feeling it.

Most of her friends at college were younger than her, carefree and full of fun, taking one-night stands in their stride. Maisie didn't think she could ever be like that, but she wished she'd guarded her heart a bit better.

At least she hadn't descended to the truly desperate—searching for Antonio when she cleaned the office or cyber-stalking him. She'd been tempted, but she kept herself from it because she told herself there was no point. And then, three weeks after she'd walked into that office, she threw up her breakfast. She didn't think too much of it, chalking it up to an unfortunate stomach bug, until it happened the next morning. And the morning after that. And her period, which was always regular, didn't come on time. It didn't come at all.

Even she, innocent that she was, or at least had been, could figure that one out. She was amazed she hadn't thought of the possibility sooner. They hadn't used protection, after all, and she wasn't dumb. Just another sign that she'd been swept away. A dangerous sign.

Maisie bought two pregnancy tests, flushing bright red as she refused to meet the young, pimply cashier's eye, and then hurried back to her studio apartment in Morningside, so far uptown you could get a nosebleed, but the only place she could afford, since Max had wanted to live with his friends from work and she had to pay the rent on her own.

She crouched in the tiny toilet as she took the first test, her heart somersaulting in her chest. She couldn't be pregnant. She just couldn't be. And yet she knew she could. She knew how life could change in a split second, everything you'd been counting on swept away like so many sandcastles.

Sitting there, the test turned over until she'd waited the allotted three minutes, she felt the same surreal sensation she'd felt when her life had changed before—in the emergency room, when the surgeon on call had informed her that her parents hadn't pulled through, and then, two weeks later, when the lawyer had told her there wasn't any money, after all.

Both times she'd felt as if she was looking at life through a warped mirror, everything wavering and distant. And that was how she felt now, even before she turned the test over. She knew what it was going to tell her. She knew her life was going to change. Again.

Sure enough, as minute three ticked by, Maisie flipped the test over and stared down at the double pink lines, completely unsurprised. She felt a leaden weight of responsibility, along with the tiniest tendril of excitement. Having a baby would derail all her plans. Only six months into her course, and she'd almost certainly have to quit, or at least put it on serious hold. Again.

And yet she knew she could no sooner rid herself of this baby than she could have rid herself of her brother. They were both part of her. They were both reasons to keep trying and surviving.

But what on earth was she going to do about Antonio Rossi?

Eventually, because she felt she had no choice, Maisie steeled herself for the inevitable internet search she'd been trying to keep herself from. She typed in his name and blinked as his photo popped up immediately, along with a Wikipedia entry. Just seeing his face, with that faint, amused smile and those bright blue eyes, made her stomach roll right over. She sat back on her sofa and stared, as memory after memory catapulted through her senses. That smile aimed right at her. Those eyes focused and intent as he'd moved towards her…

No. She had to stop thinking that way. There was absolutely no point now. Taking a deep breath, Maisie scrolled through a dozen different search results, looking for a contact number or email address and finding so much more.

She couldn't tear her gaze away from article after article, photo after photo. Antonio Rossi, the Playboy of Milan. Antonio Rossi with a supermodel, two supermodels, a glamorous-looking actress, a bored socialite. In each photo he looked charming and relaxed, and the woman was usually wound around him, pretty and pouting.

But worse than the photos were the articles. Maisie's stomach swirled as she read about 'Ruthless Rossi', the man who made his fortune in properties, demolishing buildings, buying them out from under desperate people, and then, as a sideline, offering his consultancy services to help hostile takeovers. She read scathing editorials about how companies called in Rossi to make sure the takeovers went smoothly and the fat-cat CEOs maximised their profits. According to the press, he was an expert at looking out for the big guy and trampling all over the little people, like her.

She sat back, her mind spinning, her mouth dry, her stomach near to heaving. This was the man she'd given her virginity to, the father of her baby? A hedonistic, selfish, reckless playboy who took pleasure in destroying people's livelihoods?

He'd seem so different when they'd been together, but of course it had been one alcohol-fuelled night, made hazy by both desire and grief. She hadn't known who he really was. Of course she hadn't.

Maisie spent another week dithering about what to do, wishing she had someone she could confide in. She couldn't tell Max; he'd be horrified, and in any case she doubted the advice of a twenty-two-year-old single man intent on living it up in the city was going to be helpful. Her friends at college would roll their eyes and tell her to take care of it, and that was the one thing she knew instinctively she didn't want to do. Make it go away.

No, this baby was hers, a life inside her already starting to grow. She already loved him or her, even if she knew, all too well, the sacrifices she would be called to make. The question was, did Antonio Rossi deserve to know about his child? Could she really keep such a huge and life-changing secret from the man who'd fathered her child, even if she barely knew him, and what she knew, she didn't like?

Miserably, Maisie admitted that she couldn't…and that meant finding Antonio and telling him what she suspected would be incredibly unwelcome news.

* * *

Antonio gazed out at the pale blue sky of a spring day and wondered why he couldn't concentrate. He'd been in New York for nearly a month trying to wind down Alcorn Tech. Normally an operation such as this one would take him no more than two or three weeks. Yet it was going on four weeks and he still had work to do, although he planned to leave for Milan tomorrow anyway. He couldn't waste any more time on this side project, dismantling a company into manageable pieces. What was he still trying to prove?

For some reason, these last few weeks he'd been restless and unfocused, which irritated him because work always came first. Work defined him, justified him. And here he was, staring out of the window instead of looking down at the list from HR of employees whose jobs needed to be cut or preferably adjusted.

Expelling a low breath, Antonio rose from his chair and strolled the length of the modest office he'd chosen when he'd first arrived at Alcorn. They'd proposed installing him in the CEO's office on the top floor, but Antonio knew from experience how that looked. It was far better for him to keep a low profile as he chopped and changed. Far less worrisome for the employees, most of whom had more than a sneaking suspicion of what was going on.

Although he described his consultancy services to the CEOs who hired him as a way to save money and avoid bad press, his reasons for this side business were something else entirely. Something he kept so quiet that even the press hadn't got hold of it; a few angry journalists had painted him in stark colours as a ruthless destroyer, intent on making the most money for the richest people. And that was fine, because that was why companies hired him. He was good at what he did. So good that they didn't even realise.

His intercom buzzed and, glad of the distraction from his own circling thoughts, Antonio pressed the button to answer it.

'Yes?'

'A Miss Dobson here to see you, Mr Rossi.'

A cold finger of unease trailed along Antonio's spine and then clenched his gut. Miss Dobson. He didn't know anyone named Dobson, but he had an awful feeling who might be waiting for him.

Maisie. Maisie, whom he hadn't seen for three weeks and, unfortunately, couldn't get out of his mind. More than one night he'd woken up in a fever of dreams and desire, the scent of her on his skin, the remembered feel of her silken limbs and wild hair haunting his senses. More than one night he'd stayed late at the office, wondering if he'd stumble across her again, only to leave abruptly, knowing it was better for both of them if their paths didn't cross.

What was she doing here? What did she want from him now?

'Mr Rossi?'

'I'm not available,' Antonio said shortly, suppressing the pang of guilty regret that assailed him. The last thing he needed was Maisie Dobson's questions or heaven forbid, her tears. He had a job to do, and he needed to do it. Their one night had been simply that—one night. It wasn't going anywhere. It couldn't.

'Very good, Mr Rossi,' the receptionist said after a tiny pause, and Antonio disconnected the call. It was better this way. It had to be. He didn't have anything to offer Maisie, and the sooner she forgot him, the better. The sooner he forgot her, the better, as well.

In fact, Antonio told himself grimly as he sat back down at his desk, he already had.

Three hours later he strolled through the lobby, scrolling

through the messages on his phone, when a halting voice stopped him in his tracks.

'Antonio?'

He looked up, amazed to see Maisie standing in front of him. Her hair surrounded her face in a reddish-gold nimbus, and her green eyes were wide and uncertain. She was wearing jeans and a jumper, her hands clutching her bag in front of her chest, almost as if it was a shield.

Everything in Antonio froze in that moment; the last thing he wanted was a scene, but he knew he couldn't afford to humour Maisie. The shame of their meeting, the way he'd become undone in her arms... No. He couldn't go there, not even in his own mind.

With that realisation crystallising inside him like a shard of ice, Antonio's gaze swept over her as he kept his expression dispassionate. 'I'm sorry...?'

'Would it be okay if we talked?' She sounded incredibly nervous, her voice little more than a whisper, her fingers white-knuckled on the strap of her bag. 'For a few minutes...?'

'Talk,' Antonio repeated. Maisie looked as if a breath would blow her away. She looked awful, he realised; her face pale and blotchy, her eyes bloodshot, her whole body seeming to emanate a deep sadness and fear. Had she been obsessing about their night together for the last three weeks? Building it up to more than it was?

He felt a lurch of guilty regret at what he was about to do, and yet he'd already chosen this route. He couldn't change it now. He wouldn't.

Besides, this was the kinder way, really. Antonio knew he could flatten her with a single word; their interaction could take no more than a few seconds and she would be finished. But she looked too fragile and frightened to take that kind of overt rejection, and he couldn't handle anything more. Taking a steadying breath, he raised his eye-brows in polite enquiry.

'I'm sorry, but do I know you?'

Maisie's eyes widened and she stiffened as if absorbing a blow. For a second she looked dazed, unable to speak. 'Know me...?'

'Have we met?' He kept his voice friendly but with the barest hint of impatience.

'You...you don't remember?'

He cocked his head to one side, letting his gaze flick over her. 'Obviously not.'

She gazed up into his face, searching for answers. Antonio kept his expression mild with effort. Perhaps he shouldn't have decided on this charade, but now he had no choice but to see it through. And, he told himself yet again, it was kinder than rejecting her in public.

'You don't remember me at all?' she said finally, still sounding incredulous.

'Clearly I don't. Why is that so difficult to believe?'

She flinched, and he bit back a pointless apology. He was trying *not* to hurt her, for heaven's sake, but she seemed insistent on taking everything to heart. 'I just... I didn't realise...' She shook her head slowly, seeming to retreat into herself.

Antonio watched her, battling regret, wanting this to be over. 'Excuse me, but I have places to be.' He started to step past her, and she caught his sleeve. Antonio froze. Really, she was too much. Didn't she recognise a brush-off when she saw one? Didn't she know when to quit?

'It's just... I wanted to tell you something...' she said, her voice so low and miserable Antonio had to strain to hear it.

'I cannot imagine what, since we've never met.'

She stared at him for a moment, something hardening

in her eyes and face. She straightened, dropping her hand from his sleeve. 'You're absolutely right,' she said, her voice touched with both bitterness and wonder. 'You're absolutely right. I have nothing to say to you. *Nothing*.' She spat the last word, shaking her head as she took a step back. For some reason Antonio found he couldn't move.

Maisie shook her head again. 'Someone once told me I was the most loving and generous person he knew.' She laughed, the sound harsh. 'At least now I know that person doesn't exist.' Antonio watched, still frozen, as she turned on her heel and walked quickly out of the building.

Antonio stood there, unable to move, his mind whirling. He took a quick, steadying breath and straightened his suit jacket. That could have gone better, but at least it was over. And if Maisie had, for a moment, filled him with doubt and regret, well, those inconvenient emotions were gone now, replaced by his usual resolve.

Perhaps he shouldn't have pretended he didn't know her, but the alternative would have been such a crushing blow that she might have fallen to pieces. Surely this was better, even if it didn't feel like it. And at least he wouldn't ever have to see her again.

He stepped into the waiting limo and leaned his head back against the luxurious leather seat, telling himself that that was a good thing. A very good thing. Even if it didn't feel like it at this moment.

CHAPTER FIVE

One year later

'TABLE FOUR NEEDS more wine.'

'I'll be right there.'

Maisie rolled her shoulders to ease the ache between them and reached for another bottle of wine from the crate by the kitchen door. Waitressing at high-end dinner parties wasn't where she'd seen herself ending up, but she was glad of the money. She needed it.

A lot had changed in the year since she'd looked down at those two pink lines. She had her daughter, for one. Ella was the most precious and wonderful thing that had ever happened to her. Maisie's pregnancy had been difficult, first with morning sickness and then with the onset of pre-eclampsia. She'd been bedridden for the last two months, and Max, her amazing brother, had stepped right up to help take care of her.

Maisie cringed to think of how she'd once felt undervalued and unappreciated by her brother. Max had been a star since she'd discovered she was pregnant. He'd taken time off work and insisted on moving in with her, leaving his friends and flatmates behind, so he could help her through her pregnancy and then with a fractious newborn.

He was babysitting Ella tonight, so she could work, and

had even volunteered to bring her to the hotel during her break so that Maisie could feed her. At three months old, Ella refused to take a bottle, and in any case Maisie didn't want to give up the delight of feeding her herself.

In fact, Max was due in another fifteen minutes or so, which meant she needed to deal with Table Four and make sure everyone was happy before taking a much-needed break. She'd been on her feet for the last three hours, and Ella had been up throughout the night before. Maisie had forgotten what a good night's sleep felt like.

She moved around the table of corpulent, smug businessmen—the dinner hosted in the hotel's ballroom was for some CEO or other—topping up their wine glasses and evading the occasional groping hand. She'd been waitressing for the last two months, a few nights a week, just to bring in some money. In that time she'd discovered that some privileged men tended to see waitresses as one step removed from prostitutes.

Maisie hardly thought she looked appealing, considering the extra ten pounds she was still carrying, as well as the dark circles under her eyes and the spit-up stain on her shoulder, but apparently millionaires, along with beggars, weren't choosers.

She was pouring a glass of wine when she heard a sudden, quick, indrawn breath. She looked up and the whole room fell away as she found herself staring into the bright blue eyes that had haunted her dreams as well as a good deal of her waking hours for the past year.

'Watch what you're doing!'

With a jolt Maisie looked down and saw she'd overfilled the wine glass. There was now a growing crimson stain on the pristine white tablecloth.

'I'm so sorry—'

'You're an idiot, is what you are,' the man snapped. His

face was red, his expression furious. 'You'll pay for my dry-cleaning bill.'

A single drop of wine had splashed onto his suit cuff, and Maisie's stomach hollowed out. She couldn't afford a hefty dry-cleaning bill. It would take up most of her wages for waitressing that night.

'I'm really very sorry…'

'And so you should be.' The man was bristling, spoiling for a fight. With a sinking sensation Maisie realised he was one of the men who had attempted to touch her knee while she'd been serving dinner; she'd moved away smartly, and he'd noticed and glowered. 'I should call the manager over,' he added, his indignation rising. 'See that you're fired. A place like this shouldn't have sloppy waitresses.'

'I think that would be a touch excessive.' Antonio's voice was light and charming, yet underneath there was a layer of steel that no one could mistake. The sound of it caused shivers to roll down Maisie's spine. Antonio. Here. He hadn't been here when she'd last served this table; surely she would have noticed.

'Especially,' he continued silkily, 'considering you have already been excessive.' He nodded towards the over-full glass. 'You're on your fourth, are you not, Bryson?'

The man puffed up, blustering. 'How dare you—?'

'Actually, there's no daring involved,' Antonio drawled. 'But I suppose it must seem audacious to you, a man who would bully a mere waitress.'

The man glowered while Maisie remained rooted to the spot, shocked beyond all bearing. It was mind-blowing enough to see Antonio here, but to have him *defend* her…

But then, he didn't know who she was. Did he? He was just being nice to a stranger, a *mere* waitress. Somehow, on top of everything else, that stung.

'I'll get you a new napkin,' Maisie murmured. She

walked away blindly, her mind blank and buzzing. What was Antonio doing in New York? She'd read in a gossip magazine that he was back in Milan, where his business was based. Had he come here to wreck another company, to ruin more people's lives? According to one stinging editorial she'd read, that was his speciality.

'Maisie.'

She froze halfway to the kitchen, Antonio's voice a low, insistent throb behind her. Then realisation flashed through her and she turned slowly.

'I'm sorry,' she said, trying to keep her voice from shaking, 'but do I know you?'

Antonio's jaw tightened and he gave a terse nod. 'I suppose I deserve that.'

'You *pretended* you couldn't remember me.' Maisie had to choke out the words. 'You're even more of a bastard than I thought you were, which is saying something.'

'What is that supposed to mean?'

'What do you think it means?' Her voice rose, and a few diners looked their way, rubbernecking in the hope of witnessing a big argument. Maisie wouldn't give them the satisfaction. She wouldn't give Antonio the satisfaction either, of seeing how much he'd affected her. How he'd devastated her, all those months ago.

She spun away, marching to the kitchen, and Antonio followed. In a narrow hallway off the ballroom he caught her arm.

'What are you doing here?' he demanded.

'What are *you* doing here?' she threw back, shaking off his arm. 'I live in New York. You don't.'

'I have business.'

'So do I.' She nodded towards the kitchen. 'So why don't you just go back to pretending you don't know me?' Hurt pulsed through her as she said the words. He'd *pretended,* and why? Because he couldn't be bothered to hear her out? One night and he'd already tired of her. Fury warred with hurt, and she chose anger because it felt stronger. She'd confessed to Antonio of feeling like a doormat, but she wouldn't be one now. 'I'm serious, Antonio. I don't want anything from you now. And if you think for a second that you can cash in a second night while you're in New York, forget it.'

He looked affronted, his eyes flashing icy fire. 'I wasn't thinking that.'

'Good.' She turned towards the kitchen, relieved that he didn't follow her. Relieved, and only the teeniest, tiniest bit disappointed, which she knew was stupid, of course she did, but she felt it anyway. Stubborn heart. Stubborn, stupid, foolish heart.

With shaking hands Maisie fetched a clean napkin and went back to Table Four, staring straight ahead, determined not to catch anyone's eye and certainly not Antonio's. In any case, he hadn't returned to the table, and the intoxicated guest who had made such a fuss had reduced his complaints to mere mutterings, which Maisie managed to ignore.

The job done, she retreated to the kitchen, her heart still thumping from her entirely unexpected encounter with Antonio. Why had he sought her out? Why ignore her in such a horrible manner a year ago, only to spring to her defence tonight? He'd always known who she was. Except of course he didn't know her at all. And she didn't know him.

And he couldn't know her… With a lurch of fear Maisie remembered that her brother was coming with Ella so she could feed her before her shift ended. He was due to arrive at the hotel in a few minutes. While Maisie doubted Antonio would barge into the kitchens in search of her, she still felt panicky at the thought of him being so near to Ella.

She'd made her decision not to tell him about their baby

when he'd claimed he didn't know her. It was a decision that a year of tabloid coverage had validated over and over again. Antonio Rossi, with his cold-hearted business deals and his string of bimbo lovers, was not the kind of father she wanted for her child. And, since he had claimed not to know her, he wouldn't know his daughter either.

'Maisie?' one of the waiting staff called. 'Your brother's here.'

With something close to relief, Maisie rushed to her brother and prised her three-month-old daughter from his arms.

'Maise? You all right?' Max frowned at her from underneath a shock of strawberry-blond hair, his hazel eyes narrowing in concern.

'I'm fine now.' Maisie pressed her cheek against Ella's as she breathed in that delicious scent of baby powder and sleepy softness.

'Did something happen?'

'No.' Max had become something of a guard dog since Maisie had fallen pregnant, her little brother often acting as if he were older than her. After she had taken care of him for so long, it felt both nice and strange to be looked after, but Maisie knew she couldn't burden Max with this. He was only twenty-three, just starting out in life. He didn't need to be saddled with a sister and a baby niece, even if he insisted he didn't mind.

'I'll feed her and then you can take her back home,' Maisie said. 'Thanks for bringing her out, Max. You're amazing.'

'So you keep telling me.' He gave her a crooked smile, concern still shadowing his eyes. 'I'll meet you out in the lobby, then?'

'Yes, in about twenty minutes.' Maisie smiled at her brother and then went to the women's bathroom of the hotel, which had a private nook with a comfy chair, perfect for nursing.

She felt herself calming down as Ella began to feed, one chubby hand resting possessively on Maisie's chest. She stroked her daughter's soft hair, her baby curls midnight-dark, the same colour as Antonio's. She had the same startling blue eyes as her father, as well; the deep indigo of the newborn stage had brightened to the piercing blue Maisie still saw in her dreams. If Antonio saw Ella, there could be no question of whose daughter she was.

A tremor of fear and, worse, uncertainty racked her at that realisation. Was it fair to keep Antonio from his own child? Part of her insisted yes, of course it was. All she knew about Antonio Rossi made her sure he would never be a good father and, more importantly, didn't care about being one. But she could not silence the small, treacherous whisper that protested against her unilateral decision, that Antonio deserved at least to know that he had a daughter...

Instinctively Maisie clutched Ella closer to her, and her daughter protested, squirming as she sought to latch on again.

'Sorry, sweetheart,' Maisie whispered, and made herself relax. In ten minutes Ella would have finished feeding and she'd give her back to Max, who would take her back to their apartment. Antonio would never know he had a child. That was the decision she had made a year ago, and she was sticking to it now. Nothing Antonio had done or said had made her want to reconsider.

Antonio paced the ballroom and lobby and even the kitchen of the hotel, looking for Maisie. Why he was looking for her, he couldn't articulate, even in the privacy of his own mind. Surely he should have let sleeping dogs lie—lie being the operative word. He'd blown his cover, calling her by her name, and that would hardly endear him to Maisie. What he didn't know was why he cared.

He hadn't spared her a thought this last year, or at least not much of one. Admittedly, he hadn't spared women much of a thought, in general. Work had taken over, as he sought to expand his empire further into America, and the few dates he'd gone on had been unsatisfactory in the extreme. Women, at least the women he dated, had started to bore and irritate him, and that was when he tended to think about Maisie. To remember their night together, in all its glory and shame.

But why was he looking for her now? He didn't want to rekindle their romance, not that Maisie would even be interested. He didn't want anything from her. He wanted to forget that that night, incredible as it had been, ever happened. Because he couldn't stand the thought of Maisie, or anyone, knowing his weakness. Seeing him exposed and needy and in pain as she had.

Antonio stood in the centre of the lobby, his mind spinning as he realised how foolish he was being. He should return to the table and the tedious dinner he'd been suffering through. And then he should stop by the bar and find a sexy, willing woman to help him forget about Maisie Dobson. Of course that was what he should do. It was what he always did.

Instead he just stood there, silently fuming at his own idiotic inability.

'Maisie.'

Antonio looked up at the sound of her name on another man's lips. The man was standing by the entrance to the hotel, a smile on his face as he held out his arms. Slowly Antonio turned and saw Maisie walking towards the man, a tremulous smile curving her lush lips, a baby nestled in her arms.

A baby.

Antonio stared as the man took the baby from her, cuddling the little bundle as he cooed down at it.

'Hey, sweetie.'

Jealousy fired through Antonio, although he couldn't even say why. So Maisie had moved on, found a boyfriend or husband, and had a baby pretty darn quick. That was fine. Of course it was. Except...

They'd spent the night together a year ago, and although Antonio wasn't an expert on babies by any means, the child nestled in the man's arms looked to be at least a few months old. Which meant...

Either Maisie had been pregnant when she'd slept with him, or had fallen pregnant immediately after. Or, he realised with a sickening rush, had become pregnant by him.

He hadn't used birth control. He'd been too drunk and emotional even to think of it at the time, and later he'd assumed Maisie must have been on the pill, since she hadn't seemed concerned. But now he remembered how she'd come to see him—how many weeks later? Two, three? She'd wanted to talk to him. She'd looked distraught. *What if she'd been pregnant?*

Why had he not considered such a possibility? Antonio retrained his shocked gaze on the man and baby, only to realise they'd already gone. Maisie had turned around and was walking back towards the ballroom, and presumably her waitressing duties. And his child might have just been hustled out of the door.

'Maisie.' His voice came out in a bark of command, and Maisie turned, her jade-green eyes widening as she caught sight of him. Then her face drained of colour, so quickly and dramatically that Antonio felt another rush of conviction. Why would she react like that if the child wasn't his?

'What are you doing here?' she asked in a low voice.

'I'm a guest at the dinner.'

'Yes, but...what do you want from me, Antonio?' She looked wretched, and more than once her gaze darted towards the doors and then back again.

'Let's talk in private.'

'You weren't so interested in doing that the last time we met,' Maisie snapped, summoning some spirit.

'Yes, I know, but things are different now.'

'They're different for me too.' She took a step backwards, her chin raised at a proud, determined angle. 'You didn't want to know me a year ago, Antonio, and now I don't want to know you. Doesn't feel very good, does it?' She gave a hollow laugh.

'This is not the time to be petty,' Antonio returned evenly. 'We need to talk.'

'No, we don't—'

'*Maisie.*' He cut her off, making her flinch. 'Is the baby mine?'

She opened her mouth and no words came out. It was all the confirmation Antonio needed. He took her by the arm and steered her away from the lobby, towards the lifts.

'Where are we going?' Maisie gasped as he stabbed the button for the lift.

The doors opened and Antonio stepped inside with Maisie. 'To my suite,' he informed her as the doors whooshed closed.

Maisie spun to face him, jerking her arm from his grasp. 'What? I'm not going anywhere with you—'

'You already are.'

'I'm meant to be back in the dining room! I'll lose my job—'

'I'll pay you myself.'

'I don't want your money,' she spat. 'And it's more than money, it's my reputation. If I walk out on this job, I might not be hired for another one.'

'If that is your utmost concern right now,' Antonio drawled coldly, 'then I think your priorities are out of order. But rest assured I will make sure your employment opportunities are not curtailed by our conversation.'

Maisie turned away, her arms folded, her whole body rigid. 'It's easy for you,' she said in a more moderate tone, but one that still conveyed her complete disdain. 'You've never had to worry about money.'

'That is not actually true, but I'll let it go.'

'How kind of you,' she retorted. 'I know what you're really like, Antonio Rossi.' The sneering certainty in her tone made him still. For a second he felt icy inside, as well as horribly exposed. She knew what he was really like. She'd seen his weakness. Hell, he'd shown it to her. Of course she knew what he was like, and he hated it.

'What I'm really like has no bearing on this matter,' he informed her. The doors to the lift opened directly onto his penthouse suite and he stepped out onto the black marble floor, the glittering lights of Manhattan visible from the floor-to-ceiling windows. 'All that matters is whether that child is mine.'

'And if she is?'

That single word—*she*—cut him to the core. 'She? I have a daughter?'

'I didn't say that.'

'You didn't need to.'

'Don't assume anything.' Maisie stared him down, her arms folded, her stance aggressive even as her chin wobbled a little bit. She was scared, and the only reason she'd be scared was if the child—this baby girl—really was his.

'Then stop playing games, and tell me the truth. Is the

baby mine?' Maisie pressed her lips together, her gaze sliding away from his. '*Maisie*. I deserve to know.'

'Why do you deserve anything?' she demanded, her voice wavering only a little. 'You pretended you didn't know me, Antonio! I came to your office—' Her voice broke and Antonio took advantage of the silence.

'Why did you come to my office, Maisie? What did you want to talk to me about that day?'

'Why did you pretend you didn't remember me when you obviously did?' Maisie flung back at him.

'It seemed easier—'

'Easier for you.'

'And easier for you. I didn't see our…relationship… going anywhere, and I didn't want to have to reject you in public.'

'Wow, what a prince.' She shook her head slowly. 'So thoughtful and charming. Really, I'm touched.'

'I admit, it was not the best idea I've ever had,' Antonio returned tightly. And it wasn't the entire truth. He'd pretended he didn't know her because he'd been so ashamed by his weakness, the weakness she'd seen. Even now it made him cringe, and then seethe. 'In any case, you still haven't answered my question.'

She remained silent, her gaze averted from his, her arms wrapped around her body as if she were holding herself together. Impatience warred with an incredulous hope. 'Maisie—'

'What do you want me to say?' she interjected quietly. 'What do you expect me to say?'

'That's why I'm asking…'

Maisie let out a shuddering sigh and then turned to him resolutely, as if facing a firing squad, the execution of all her hopes. 'Yes, Antonio,' she said, her voice sounding a note of defeat. 'The baby is yours. You have a daughter.'

CHAPTER SIX

MAISIE WATCHED THE emotions flash across Antonio's face—disbelief, shock, and then, surprisingly, wonder. Maybe even joy. A smile bloomed and then, quite suddenly, withered. His lips compressed and he folded his arms, back to being the autocratic stranger whom Maisie could fully believe was responsible for dismantling companies and destroying dreams, at least according to the reports she'd read.

'You should have told me.'

'I tried.' Surely he couldn't blame her for that. She wouldn't let him. 'You seem to have selective amnesia, don't you?' Maisie added, her indignation turning her uncharacteristically caustic. 'I came to your office, I asked if we could talk. You didn't want to know.'

'I would have agreed to a discussion if I'd known—'

'Sorry I wasn't willing to drop that bombshell in the middle of a crowded lobby,' Maisie fired back, properly furious now. 'If you'd had the barest modicum of decency, you would have given me a hearing. Two seconds of your time, at least. But maybe that's more than you give most women. It certainly seems so, based on the articles I've seen in the tabloids.'

Antonio's lips curled, his eyes flashing fire. 'You shouldn't read tabloids. They're nothing but rubbish.'

'A lot of rubbish is written about you, then.'

He shrugged his powerful shoulders. 'I don't read those rags.'

'I didn't either, until they proved to be the only way to find out what kind of man you are.'

His lips compressed, his whole body stilling. 'And you decided what kind of man I am from gossip magazines?'

'And from your own actions. Nothing you did or said made me think you'd welcome a child, Antonio.'

'But I still should have known.'

Maisie shrugged back at him, refusing to apologise for his own lamentable shortcomings. 'Like I said, I tried.'

'You should have tried harder,' Antonio flashed back. He took a steadying breath and squared his shoulders. 'But that doesn't matter now. What matters is the future. Our future.'

Maisie didn't miss the emphasis, and it sent a clear, cold note of fear twanging through her. 'What do you mean, our future?'

'Do you think now that I know I have a child, a daughter, I'm going to turn my back on her? Walk away as if nothing has changed?'

'Frankly I don't know what you're going to do,' Maisie said, struggling to keep her voice even. What was Antonio going to want? Demand? Because her life was just about on a steady keel, and she really couldn't stand the boat being rocked. Yet in that moment she feared Antonio was going to tip it right over and capsize her fledgling happiness.

'Then I'll tell you,' Antonio said, his voice turning inexorable. 'I'm going to be involved in my child's life.'

'How?' A headache had begun to flicker at Maisie's temples. She wasn't emotionally ready to have this conversation. Less than an hour ago she hadn't thought she'd ever see Antonio Rossi again, and now she was in his hotel suite while he made demands.

And demands they definitely were, because everything about Antonio radiated power. Authority. Charisma. She knew so much about him that she hated, from his business dealings to his bedroom ones, and yet even now she could not deny the magnetic pull he had on her. Even now she couldn't keep from noticing the ice-blue of his eyes, the strong line of his jaw, the ink-dark hair that flopped over his forehead and made her remember how she'd run her fingers through it.

She couldn't keep her gaze from dropping to that long, lithe body that she'd felt against her own. His crisp white tuxedo shirt was the perfect foil for his bronzed skin and blue eyes. He looked magnificent, intimidating, and totally out of her league. She could hardly believe he'd been hers for a night, although of course he hadn't been. Not really. And what did he want with her now?

Nothing, she quickly found out. 'We'll have joint custody,' Antonio informed her curtly, as if it was a simple and glaringly obvious matter. Maisie gaped.

'Joint? How? You live in Milan and I live in New York. I'm her mother, Antonio. She's only three months old—'

'And I've missed those first three months. I won't miss any more.'

Maisie had had no idea what to expect from Antonio, but it definitely hadn't been this. 'You don't seem like someone who wants a child,' she remarked numbly.

'This isn't a question of want, it's one of duty. Responsibility.'

'Ella is not just a duty—'

'Ella? Is that her name?'

Maisie lifted a chin, torn between wishing she hadn't mentioned her daughter's name and knowing that all of this was painfully necessary. 'Yes.'

'Ella,' Antonio repeated softly. An emotion flashed

across his face, too quickly for Maisie to discern what it was, and then he swung away so he was staring at the twinkling lights of the city, his back to her.

'She can spend half the year with me, and half the year with you.'

Maisie's heart started to splinter. '*Half* the year? You'd deprive me of my child for six months?'

'I can ask you the same.'

'Antonio, you work full-time. You travel the world. How on earth would you care for her, especially when she's so small?' Terror dug its poisonous claws into Maisie's heart and held on. She *couldn't* let this happen, and yet how could she fight it? Antonio was Ella's father, and he was far more powerful than she was. She couldn't fight him, but she would try with everything she had.

Antonio didn't answer her breathless question, and desperation made Maisie press the point. 'It's not reasonable. You'd have to hire a nanny, when she could be with her mother, the person who loves her most—'

'You work.'

'Only the occasional evening, and Max looks after her.'

'Max?'

Was she imagining the needle-like note of jealousy that had entered his voice? 'My brother. You remember I told you about him? Or did he not make the cut of what you choose to remember and to forget?'

'I remember you talking about your brother.' He turned away, seeming to want to close the conversation.

'And I remember you talking about yours,' Maisie said, compelled to a painful honesty she hadn't expected either to give or receive. Not now, with their history so fraught and fragmented. Yet for one brief, breathless moment she remembered how close she'd felt to him, how emotionally connected. Had it all been a mirage? A lie?

'Don't.' Antonio's voice was rough, his body angled away from her. 'Let's not talk about that. The past is exactly that. We need to focus on the future.'

'So you said, but we can't make these kinds of life-changing decisions in the course of one evening.' Maisie took a steadying breath, willing the panic she'd felt swimming through her mind to recede a little.

Antonio knew about his daughter and, despite the fear she still felt, it was, in some ways, a relief. No more wondering. No more hiding the truth. It was out, and now they both had to deal with it. She'd see that as a good thing when she'd recovered from the shock. She'd have to.

'Maybe not in the course of an evening,' Antonio said levelly as he turned around to face her, 'but soon. I leave for Milan in three days.'

Maisie only just stopped herself from rolling her eyes. 'And finding out you have a daughter won't keep you from changing your plans? What a great start.'

His mouth compressed, his eyes turning flinty. 'It's not like that.'

'It seems like it is.'

'I'm not going to argue with you about this now,' Antonio said, his tone growing impatient. 'You're right, in that we can't discuss or decide everything tonight.'

'Exactly.' Maisie exhaled in relief. At least they were in agreement about that.

'I'll escort you home, then pick you up in the morning to continue our discussion.'

That made him sound a little bit like her jailer. 'Is that really necessary—?'

'Yes.' Antonio cut her off. 'It is.' He slid his mobile phone out of his breast pocket and thumbed a quick text. 'My car will be waiting outside.'

'I'm supposed to work until the party is over...'

'The party is over,' Antonio said flatly, and Maisie was pretty sure he wasn't talking about the dinner downstairs. Yes, the party was over. But what came next?

Maisie didn't say a word as she and Antonio rode down in the lift together. He glanced at her out of the corner of his eye, trying to assess her mood. Would she be compliant? Would she fight? And, most importantly, what the hell did he really want?

Ella's birth, her existence, had blindsided him. He hadn't been able to think properly, and still couldn't. His gut reaction, the kneejerk response he hadn't been able to suppress or moderate, had been that his daughter was his and he wanted her right now. For ever.

The strength and intensity of his emotion surprised him. He'd never wanted children or marriage, because he'd seen first-hand the negative and destructive elements of both. Yet here he was, contemplating at least one of them. The trouble was, he really couldn't see how it was going to work.

Maisie had pointed out just a few of the complications— the distance between them, and the hectic pace of his work life. Besides, a child, and especially a baby, needed her mother. Still, he'd figure those things out eventually. The most important matter had already been settled; he would be in Ella's life. He needed to be.

Out in the street, the spring air was balmy, the streets empty of traffic. A limo idled at the kerb, and the driver hopped out as soon as he saw Antonio.

'Sir.'

'Thank you, Carl.' He used the same driver every time he came to New York, which was usually once or twice a year. He hadn't been back since he'd been with Maisie, something that caused him a flicker of regret and wonder.

Would he have run into her, if he'd come back? Sought her out? Perhaps he wouldn't have missed the first three months of his daughter's life.

His daughter. The words felled him, flayed him. He couldn't believe it. He couldn't believe he felt so strongly about it, about his child and his fatherhood, and yet he did. He knew he did.

Maisie slid inside the limo and scooted to the far side, practically pressing herself against the door in her desire to escape him.

Antonio slid in next to her, closing the door behind him. The limo pulled smoothly into the street, and Maisie turned her face to the window.

'Where do you live?' Antonio asked.

'In Inwood, on Two Hundred and Eighth Street.' She gave him the rest of the address, and he arched an eyebrow.

'I didn't realise the street numbers went up that high.'

'Most people don't think of it as part of Manhattan,' Maisie acknowledged, her manner thawing slightly. 'But the rent is cheap.'

Antonio frowned. He hated the thought that Maisie, and therefore his daughter, had struggled for money while he'd remained ignorant. As the limo sped uptown he realised how little he knew about the mother of his child. He barely knew anything at all.

'Are you still in school?' he asked abruptly, and Maisie turned to him, surprised.

'No. I had to give up my course when I was pregnant with Ella.'

'What course was it?'

She pressed her lips together, something inside her seeming to shutter. 'Violin performance at Juilliard.'

That surprised him. He'd been expecting her to be doing some mundane and practical course at a community college, not playing an instrument at one of the best music schools in the world. She'd given up a lot for their child. 'Will you go back to it?'

'I don't think so.'

'Why not?'

She shrugged. 'It's too difficult with Ella, and in any case, I'm not sure I'm cut out for that high-pressure environment.'

More things he didn't know about her. His curiosity suddenly seemed insatiable, and yet also inconvenient. He didn't want to have some sort of pseudo-relationship with Maisie, simply because they shared a child. Even though he was a father now, Antonio knew he wasn't cut out for marriage, and certainly not for love. So what the hell was he going to do?

They didn't talk for the rest of the trip uptown, the streets getting more rundown the farther north they went. Finally Maisie indicated that the driver should turn, and a few seconds later Carl pulled up in front of a shabby-looking brick building, the paint peeling from the fire-escape stairs, a drift of take-away menus and junk mail piled up in front of the door.

'You live here?' He couldn't keep the censure from his voice. This was no place to raise a child, or at least his child.

'Yes.' Maisie glanced at him, both wary and affronted. 'It's fine. There are a lot of families in this neighbourhood.' She opened the door, about to get out. 'You don't have to see me to the door—'

'I'll see you all the way to your apartment,' Antonio returned. 'I want to know where you live.'

'It's late, Antonio—'

'And we're already here.' He slid out his own side, then strode around to help her out of the limo. She looked as if she wanted to refuse to take his hand, but then with a little sigh she did. Even now, with so much going on, Antonio felt the silken slide of her fingers against his palm and his gut tightened with both desire and memory.

He dropped her hand as soon as she'd straightened, and Maisie fished for her keys in her purse while the limo idled and Antonio waited impatiently.

She opened the door and stepped aside for him to go through; the lobby of the building was dark and cramped and smelled of old fried food.

'There's no lift?' he demanded as she started up the stairs.

'No,' Maisie answered tiredly, 'and we live on the sixth floor, so I hope you're in good shape.'

'We?'

'My brother Max and me.'

They climbed the five flights of narrow stairs in silence, Antonio's unease deepening with every floor.

'How did you manage those stairs when you were pregnant?' he demanded as they reached the top floor.

'I didn't move here until after Ella was born, but in any case I was bedridden for the last two months of my pregnancy.'

'Bedridden?' Shocked alarm rippled through him. 'Why?'

'I had pre-eclampsia. Ella was born three weeks early by emergency Caesarean section as a result.'

And he'd had no idea about any of it. 'You should have got in touch with me. I could have helped.'

'You didn't want to know,' Maisie reminded him, but she sounded tired rather than angry about it. Guilt bit deep. He knew Maisie was right. It was his own fault for blanking Maisie when he should have listened to her.

'I'm sorry,' he said, his voice low.

She turned to him in surprise. 'Wow, an apology. Something I didn't realise you were capable of.'

Antonio stiffened. 'I am certainly capable of apologising when needed—'

'Do you apologise to all the people whose jobs you cut?'

His eyes narrowed. 'Is that what you think—?'

'One newspaper nicknamed you "The Destroyer".'

'Like I said, I wouldn't pay attention to tabloids.'

Maisie folded her arms across her chest. 'Do you deny it?'

'Now is not the time to talk about my business.' He refused to explain himself or his actions. He certainly wasn't going to justify them. 'Why don't you open the door?'

'All right, but please be quiet. Ella is a very light sleeper.'

'Fine.'

Maisie unlocked the door and stepped into the small living room. It was a shabby but homey room, with a couple of armchairs and a sofa. Baby toys were scattered across a throw rug on the floor. Her brother was sprawled asleep on the sofa and he started awake as they came in.

'Maisie…' His mouth dropped open as he took in Antonio standing behind his sister. 'Who is this?'

'It's fine, Max.' Maisie took a deep breath and dropped her bag and keys on a table by the door. 'This is Antonio, Ella's father.'

'Ella's—'

'He's leaving now.'

'I want to see her first.' His voice throbbed with urgency.

Maisie turned to him, fear in her eyes. 'She's asleep—'

'I'll be quiet. Don't deny me this, Maisie. I haven't even seen my own daughter yet.' He paused, his gaze boring into hers. 'Please.'

Pain flashed across Maisie's face. Why was she so reluctant to let him into Ella's life? What was she so afraid of?

I know what kind of man you are. Antonio's gut cramped at the memory. Maisie knew too much, and that was why she kept him at a distance. Yet he couldn't let his own failures and weaknesses stand in the way of a relationship with his daughter. That much he knew—in his bones, and in his heart.

'All right,' Maisie said quietly, and she beckoned him down a narrow hall, pausing outside the door. 'Please be quiet,' she whispered.

'I said I would.'

Maisie pushed the door open with her fingertips and then tiptoed in, Antonio following behind, holding his breath. The room was small, its limited space taken up by a double bed and a cot next to it. Antonio's gaze took in the rumpled duvet on the bed and the feminine pyjamas crumpled on the floor, before he trained it on the tiny, perfect form in the cot.

He crept forward, his heart pounding hard as he looked down at his daughter. She lay on her back, one tiny fist flung up by her face, her wispy baby curls as dark as his own hair, sable lashes feathering her plump cheeks. If Antonio had had any notion to confirm his fatherhood with a paternity test, it evaporated in view of Ella. She was so very clearly his, from the dark hair to the tiny cleft in her chin. Her breath came out in a sigh, and Antonio's heart clenched with love, painful but good. So good.

'Ella.' He whispered it, just to hear the name on his tongue. To claim ownership, or at least begin to. Gently he reached down and with one fingertip he stroked her soft, round cheek.

'Antonio…'

'She's still asleep.' He glanced at Maisie standing next to the cot, her hands clasped together as she chewed her lip. She looked uncertain and fearful but also emotional.

The three of them were a family, whether they wanted to be or not. That much Antonio knew.

Slowly he backed away from the cot, and Maisie followed him out of the room. Back in the living room Max was standing by the tiny alcove kitchen, looking mutinous. Maisie just looked tired.

'I'll go now,' Antonio said shortly. 'But I'll be back tomorrow.'

'Tomorrow—'

'We have much to discuss, Maisie. You know that.' She acknowledged this with a jerky nod of her head. 'I'll pick you and Ella up at ten in the morning,' Antonio told her. 'And then we'll start making decisions.' His tone was final and commanding, and Maisie flinched as she nodded again, her chin jutted out at a stubborn angle, but she didn't disagree.

Antonio glanced at Max, who was glaring at him, and then back at Maisie. 'I'll see you tomorrow,' he said. As he left he didn't know whether it had been a threat or a promise, or which Maisie had taken it as.

CHAPTER SEVEN

MAISIE PLACED ELLA, just fed and content at least for a few minutes, on a soft pink blanket before hurrying around in a pointless attempt to tidy up the apartment's tiny living space.

She'd barely slept last night, her mind racing from all the revelations, spinning in constant circles as she tried to second-guess what Antonio would want. How much he would demand. And how much she would be willing to give, although whether she'd have any choice was another matter.

Max had wanted answers from her, but she'd been too tired and overwhelmed to explain. Before he'd gone to work this morning, he'd insisted that she not make any rash decisions. 'We can consult a lawyer, Maisie. This Antonio guy doesn't have all the power.'

'But he is Ella's father, Max,' Maisie said quietly. 'I can't deny him access to his daughter on moral grounds, never mind legal ones.' Which left her with a sinking sensation in the pit of her stomach. Would Antonio really insist that he have Ella for half the year? It seemed inconceivable, and yet she knew he was 'Ruthless Rossi'. The man was capable of anything, and he had destroyed lives without so much as a flicker of an eyelid. One article had detailed the five hundred jobs he'd ruthlessly cut when a company had hired him to manage a hostile takeover.

Ella started to stir and fuss just as the doorbell rang. Maisie straightened, sparing her flustered reflection a single glance in the mirror. Her face was flushed, her hair wilder than usual, and she had not one but two stains on the fresh sweater she'd put on that morning.

Grimacing, she went to the intercom and buzzed Antonio up. As soon as he entered the room she felt the need to take a step back, to draw a breath. He was so *much*. Had he always been this tall, looked this strong? He wore a navy-blue suit with a paler blue shirt and a cobalt tie that made his eyes look even bluer. Everything about him was sharp and magnetic and powerful.

He smelled of the woodsy aftershave Maisie remembered from a year ago, and just like that she was back in that darkened office, her body at his delicious mercy. That was the last thing she wanted to be thinking of now.

From her place on the blanket Ella let out a cry of protest at being ignored, and Maisie went to scoop her up, grateful for the distraction.

'What's wrong with her?' Antonio asked as Ella continued to fuss.

'Nothing's wrong with her. She's just a baby. That's how they are.'

'Hmm.' Antonio surveyed her, Ella cradled against her chest. 'I don't know anything about babies, to be honest.'

'I didn't, either, before Ella,' Maisie admitted with a wry laugh. 'It's been a steep learning curve.'

'I'm sure.' He thrust his hands in the pockets of his trousers, looking ill at ease and incongruous in her tiny, shabby apartment. Maisie stroked Ella's downy hair, wondering what had driven Antonio to step up as a father. It seemed, she had to admit, a little out of character.

'So has it sunk in?' she asked after a moment, once Ella had settled down. 'That you're a father?'

'I don't know if it will ever sink in properly.' He shook his head slowly. 'I suppose it should have crossed my mind, considering we didn't use birth control.'

A blush stole over her cheeks at the blatant reminder of that one life-changing and emotional night. 'I suppose we had other things on our minds.'

'I assumed you were on the pill, but obviously that was not an assumption I should have made.' He rubbed his jaw, clearly uncomfortable. 'I'm just trying to explain why it didn't cross my mind that you could have fallen pregnant.'

'I don't have an explanation,' Maisie answered with a laugh, trying to lighten the mood. Already her body felt prickly and oversensitive, flashes of memory from that night going through her mind like streaks of lightning. She shifted Ella to her other shoulder. 'Naivety, perhaps.'

Antonio frowned. 'Naivety?'

Maisie's blush deepened, and she considered bluffing it out, but then decided it didn't matter any more. She wasn't about to invent some imaginary string of lovers to save face. 'I hadn't had many, or any, experiences of one-night stands, or anything like that. Birth control had never been an issue.'

'Why not?'

Was he really so dense that he couldn't figure out what she was saying? Fine, then she would spell it out. 'Because I was a virgin, Antonio.'

Antonio's expression froze for a second, and then his brows snapped together, his eyes piercingly bright as they arrowed in on her. 'A *virgin*?' He sounded completely incredulous.

'Yes.' She laughed, shaking her head. 'You sound surprised. I thought you might have realised, I suppose. Can't men tell? I thought you'd have guessed at least, because I was so clumsy.'

'You weren't clumsy.'

'I felt like it. I had no idea what I was doing.' She turned away, embarrassed by how frank they were both being, as well as how many memories were rushing through her, a tangle of sensual images that made her pulse start to skyrocket. 'Anyway, that's why I didn't think about birth control.'

Antonio was silent for a tense moment. 'I didn't realise you were a virgin,' he said at last.

'It doesn't matter.'

'It does,' he insisted in a low voice. 'If I'd known...'

'What?' She tried for light and missed, but something kept her going. 'You wouldn't have touched me? You would have found a bed? Lit a couple of candles?'

'I don't know,' Antonio admitted. 'But it would have made a difference.'

'It's all in the past now, and we don't need to discuss it or even think of it any more,' Maisie said as firmly as she could. 'What we need to think about is Ella, and what's best for her.'

'I agree. And what is best for her is surely to live with both of her parents.'

Maisie's heart lurched at his implacable tone. 'And how is that meant to happen?'

Ella had started to fuss again, and without even realising it Maisie began to do the jiggling and deep knee-bend routine that she'd discovered, through many fraught and sleepless nights, helped her daughter to settle.

'What are you doing?' Antonio asked, his eyebrows raised in incredulity.

He was looking at her as if she was mad, and Maisie supposed she did look a little strange, jiggling Ella about while she performed squats.

'It helps her settle.'

'How did you figure that one out?'

'Trial and error.'

Antonio's expression softened, surprising her. 'It sounds like it's been challenging.'

'It has, but I wouldn't change a thing. Not even for a second.'

'I believe you.' He glanced around the living room again, and then back to her. Maisie watched him warily, unsure what was coming. 'Why don't we go out? It's a beautiful spring day. Does Ella have a pram?'

'A stroller, yes. She likes being in it usually.'

'All the better. We can talk as we walk. Is there a park near by?'

'Fort Tryon Park isn't too far away,' Maisie suggested. 'I sometimes take Ella there.'

'Right, then, that's what we'll do.' Antonio gave a decisive nod. 'What can I do to help you get her ready?'

It felt entirely surreal and strange to be strolling down one of the neighbourhood's wide avenues towards the leafy green park in the distance, Maisie next to him, Ella in her pram. Did the people glancing their way think they were a family? *Were* they?

It was so odd. For ten years, since his brother's death, Antonio had kept himself solitary. Yes, he'd had flings and affairs, but no one had ever meant anything to him. No one had come close enough to know him. Until Maisie.

That night she'd slipped under his defences and it was what had made him pretend he didn't know her. What had kept him tossing and turning last night, wondering how he could honour his responsibility to his daughter—which he intended to do utterly—and still keep Maisie at a safe distance. He needed to somehow find a way.

They strolled through the park, along winding paths

and through verdant meadows and copses of trees, the sun shining high above them. Perched on a craggy outlook was a medieval-looking building Antonio had never seen before.

'It's part of the Metropolitan Museum of Art,' Maisie explained when he asked. 'A reconstructed medieval monastery called the Cloisters.'

As they walked along, Ella kicked her chubby legs in the stroller as she blinked up at the sunshine.

'She likes the movement, I think,' Maisie said. 'She always wants to be moving, whether it's me jiggling her or in her stroller. She loves riding on the bus.'

'Tell me about her,' Antonio urged, the need to know more about his daughter nearly overwhelming. 'Your pregnancy and her birth; everything.'

Maisie glanced at him in surprise. 'I thought you wanted to talk about the future?'

'First I want to know about the past.'

'All right,' she said slowly, and then she began to tell him all the things he'd missed, all the things he hadn't even realised had been happening. Her debilitating morning sickness, which she tried to make light of, but which Antonio could tell had been horrible; the onset of pre-eclampsia in the third trimester.

'My ankles swelled up like balloons,' Maisie said with a grimace. 'I felt awful. That's when I left school.'

'Do you miss it?'

She paused, pursing her lips in thought. 'Honestly? Not as much as I thought I would. Not as much as I feel I should, and that makes me feel guilty.'

'Why?'

She shrugged. 'Because it was all I was working towards. Taking care of Max, making sure he got to go to college, keeping us afloat… The whole time going to Juilliard was what drove me. I'd finally get there one day, and then everything would make sense somehow. But it didn't quite feel like that.'

'What did it feel like?'

Maisie let out a little laugh. 'You really want to know this?'

'Yes,' Antonio answered, the word surprisingly heart-felt. 'Yes, I do.'

They were walking along a path high above the Hudson River, and Maisie glanced down at the water glinting and sparkling below, her forehead creased in thought. 'It felt like instead of arriving at the top of the mountain, I was at the bottom. And this time there were lots of other climbers, elbowing each other out of the way.' She sighed and shook her head. 'The truth is, I'm just not cut out for that kind of competitive, cut-throat environment. Everyone else put performance first in their lives, and I've always put people first. I couldn't make the change.'

'Perhaps that doesn't have to be negative.'

'It isn't,' Maisie declared with a spark of challenge. 'Of course it isn't. I made a choice willingly, deliberately. I'll never regret taking care of Max, and I certainly don't re-gret this little one.' She gazed down at Ella, her face soft-ening in love as she looked at her daughter. Ella's eyelids were fluttering closed, one tiny fist flung up by her face.

Antonio gazed in rapture and wonder at his daughter, and then back at Maisie. She still looked pale and tired, but also very lovely with the sun gilding her hair in gold, wild curls dancing about her heart-shaped face. The freckles he remembered from before were scattered across her nose. Her figure had been made softer and rounder by mother-hood, and she seemed more womanly, and yes, more al-luring.

Even now, especially now, Antonio desired her. Knowing she had brought his child into the world only piqued his desire rather than lessened it, a fact which was both undeniable and inconvenient.

Maisie's expression turned serious as she gazed down at Ella. 'But what we really need to talk about is the future, Antonio.' She drew a quick breath. 'I know it's a shock to discover you have a daughter, and I applaud your instinct to take responsibility—'

'Applaud?' Antonio repeated. He didn't like the sound of that. He saw how Maisie's mouth had compressed, her eyes narrowing, her body stiff. She looked as if she was squaring up for a fight.

'You want to do the right thing—'

'You make me sound so noble,' Antonio drawled. 'Really, I'm overwhelmed.'

'What I'm trying to say is, I get it.'

'I really don't think you do.'

She sighed impatiently, brushing a strand of red-gold hair away from her face. 'Look, there's no way Ella could ever fit into your life, not properly. And it's not fair of you to demand joint custody just because you feel it's the right thing to do, or maybe because you're mad at me for keeping her from you—'

'You think I would ask for joint custody simply out of some kind of revenge?' Her opinion of him continued to fall, it seemed, and yet he could hardly blame her.

'Maybe not quite revenge, but…' Maisie hesitated, then lifted her chin, her emerald eyes flashing. 'Antonio, you're known as a ruthless businessman. You're nicknamed "The Destroyer"! You take apart buildings and companies and dismantle people's lives without a flicker of regret or compassion.'

'You've seen me at work, then?' Antonio said. He felt cold with a sudden rage but also, he realised with a twinge of shame, with hurt. He didn't like that she had such a low of opinion of him, but he would not stand here and defend himself against such baseless accusations.

And were they really baseless?

Maisie thought she knew him from his business, but she didn't at all. *And yet...* And yet she knew him all too well. It was an impossible situation, and a tiny, treacherous part of him was tempted to walk away. Easier all around, and Ella would be well cared for.

But he couldn't do that. He couldn't just abandon his daughter. Maybe it would be the best thing, he acknowledged grimly, because heaven knew he didn't have the best example of a father to follow, but he still wanted to try, whatever that looked like. Felt like.

Except right now it seemed as if Maisie didn't want him to.

'Of course I haven't seen you at work,' Maisie said, two spots of colour appearing high on her cheeks, 'but I've heard—'

'Judged without a trial,' Antonio remarked sardonically. 'You read an article or two, I suppose, most of them written by journalists who will create dirt when they can't dig it up?'

'Are you saying you didn't knock down an apartment building in Rome that houses a thousand low-income residents?'

His mouth compressed as he stared at her. 'You've done your homework, I see.'

'You don't deny it?'

'That I knocked the building down? No.' It had been a fire hazard and a death trap. But he wasn't going to trip over himself explaining.

She nodded slowly, as if he'd confirmed her worst suspicions. 'In any case, Antonio, you can't deny your lifestyle—working all hours, a different woman every week, most of them looking as if they've only got a handful of brain cells.'

'You're sounding quite judgemental—'

'The point is,' she cut across him determinedly, 'your life isn't suitable for raising a child.'

He took a slow, even breath, mainly to keep hold of his temper. She had a point. Of course she did. And it was absolutely idiotic of him to feel hurt by it all. He hadn't had a serious romantic relationship in his entire life. 'What if I'm willing to change?'

She looked incredulous. '*Are* you?'

'Why shouldn't I be?' Antonio retorted, nettled despite his best efforts not to be. 'You obviously were. Do I have to be so different?'

'Antonio, we *are* different.' She looked a bit exasperated and also far too sad. Antonio looked away so she couldn't see the guilt on his face. They were different; as far as he could tell, she'd saved her brother, while he'd ruined his. And he had no idea if he was able to change, never mind whether he wanted to or not.

When he considered all that, he didn't deserve to be in her life, or demand to be in his daughter's life. And yet to walk away felt intolerable. Impossible. Here was a chance, if not for redemption, then at least for atonement.

'We're not that different,' he said stubbornly, even though he knew it was a lie. They were completely different. Even during their one night together, he'd seen Maisie Dobson for what she was—an open, generous, loving person. Someone who would put another's life before her own. So, so different from him.

Maisie stared at him for a moment, the freckles standing

out on her nose as her face paled. 'So what do you want, then?' she asked slowly, and he knew the question cost her.

'I want,' Antonio answered with slow deliberation, 'for you and Ella to come with me to Milan.'

CHAPTER EIGHT

'*MILAN?*'

Maisie could do no more than gape for a few soundless seconds as Antonio levelled her with a look that was both implacable and assured.

'You mean,' Maisie finally said, struggling to get her thoughts straight, 'you want us to visit…?'

'No, to live.' Antonio folded his arms. 'It's the only option that makes sense.'

'How on earth does that make sense?' Maisie's voice had risen and Ella stirred in her stroller.

'How does it not?' Antonio countered, and Ella started to cry.

He looked so stricken, as if it was his fault, that Maisie almost smiled despite the shock and terror battering her senses.

'She's just hungry, I need to feed her.'

'Then why don't we go somewhere more comfortable, such as my hotel suite? I have a limo waiting by your apartment.'

Maisie hesitated, unsure whether she wanted to negotiate with Antonio on his turf, as she had been last night, but also recognising that she needed to choose her battles. This certainly wasn't a crucial one, whereas moving to Milan was. She'd save her strength for that.

'All right,' she relented. 'But we'd better go quickly. Ella doesn't like to wait for her dinner.'

Antonio took control of the stroller as they hurried back towards her apartment, a limo meeting them right outside the park. Fifteen minutes later they were pulling up in front of the luxurious hotel where Maisie had waitressed last night, which felt like a lifetime ago. Then they were soaring up to the penthouse suite, a fussy Ella clutched to Maisie's chest.

She stepped into the suite, amazed at the sheer opulence of the place she had been too stunned to notice last night. Antiques and expensive art vied for space on the walls and floor, and competed with the floor-to-ceiling windows that afforded a view of the city.

'This is amazing,' Maisie said with a little, incredulous laugh. She'd waitressed in plenty of luxury hotels but apart from last night she'd never been in one of the guest rooms, never mind the penthouse suite. 'Do you always stay in places like this?' Antonio shrugged in reply. Of course he did. This was the norm for him. They really were from completely different worlds. And yet it seemed Antonio wanted her to join his. But Maisie knew she wasn't ready to think about that yet, not when Ella was hungry and grizzly and everything felt so precarious and strange.

'What do you need?' Antonio asked, nodding towards their daughter.

'Just a quiet space and a comfy chair,' Maisie answered. 'And maybe a glass of water.'

'I can manage all those things,' Antonio said with a small smile, and something inside Maisie lightened. This felt strange, but it also felt the tiniest bit nice, being taken care of.

A few minutes later she was sitting comfortably in a squashy armchair in one of the suite's bedrooms, Ella guzzling happily at her breast. Outside the city stretched out, Central Park a haze of green in the distance. Maisie leaned her head back against the chair and closed her eyes—she hadn't slept much last night.

A sound startled her out of her doze. She opened her eyes to see Antonio standing in the doorway, a glass of water in his hand and an odd expression on his face.

Belatedly Maisie realised how exposed she was, her shirt hiked up so Ella could nurse.

'Sorry,' she said, uncertain if she should apologise.

'There's nothing to be sorry for.' Antonio crossed the room to place the glass of water on the table beside her. 'It's a lovely sight.'

'It feels like she's always hungry.' Maisie lowered her gaze as she stroked her daughter's head.

Antonio frowned. 'Always hungry and never sleeping. It sounds as if she makes many demands.'

'She's just a normal baby,' Maisie protested. 'I don't mean to complain.'

'You aren't. I'm just concerned for you. You look tired.'

Maisie prickled instinctively. 'If you're implying that I can't manage—'

'Maisie, I am implying no such thing. Why do you think I want you to come to Milan? Because Ella needs you.'

Maisie leaned her head back against the chair. She knew they had to talk about Milan—that was why she was here in his hotel suite—but she felt as if she couldn't even begin to get her head around it.

'Antonio, how can I just move to Milan?'

'Easily.'

'I don't even have a visa.'

'That could be arranged.'

For a man like him, undoubtedly. Still her mind spun. 'What would I do? I don't even speak Italian.'

'Many people speak English, and you could learn Italian. I'd be happy to provide a tutor.'

He was dealing with her concerns as soon as she'd verbalised them, but that still wasn't enough. The whole thing was impossible. Unfathomable. And the last thing she wanted was for Antonio to brush aside her concerns, to treat them as if they weren't important. The last thing she wanted, she acknowledged hollowly, was to feel like this man's doormat.

But what if it's best for your daughter?

'I can't,' she said firmly. 'I have a life here in New York.'

Antonio cocked an eyebrow. 'Yet your only work is waitressing a few nights a week, and you've dropped out of school.'

Stung, she snapped, 'That's not my whole life. I have friends, my brother, a *life*. Maybe it doesn't seem like much to you, but—'

'I'm not saying that, Maisie. Only that perhaps you could consider a change, for the sake of our child.'

He made it all sound so reasonable, but Maisie knew it wasn't. Of course it wasn't. How could it be? People didn't just move countries without knowing a soul, or having a job, simply because someone said they should.

'I can't afford to move. I can barely afford the rent on my apartment as it is.'

Antonio drew back, affronted. 'Of course I would pay for all your expenses, including your accommodation.'

Now, that was the first thing that sounded tempting. Not having to worry about money for the first time in for ever? And yet, to be dependent on one person, a man she didn't know and certainly didn't trust. A man who didn't seem to be very concerned with her, just her—their—daughter.

'You're asking a lot of me,' she said after a moment.

'For Ella's sake.'

Maisie glanced down at their daughter. She'd fallen asleep, her rosebud lips slackening, her dark eyelashes fanning her plump, pink cheeks. She was beautiful, and Antonio had never even held her. Could she really be so unfair, so unreasonable, to deny him his daughter? Yet how could the alternative be to move to another country?

'There has to be some compromise.'

'Where? In the middle of the Atlantic?'

'What about when she's older…?'

'So I'm completely absent from her early life?'

'You could visit…'

'I don't want to be some sort of doting stranger, Maisie,' Antonio snapped, a savage note entering his voice. 'I'm her *father*.'

She stared at him helplessly, swamped by guilt and uncertainty. 'Can I think about it?' she asked at last.

'I leave for Milan in two days.'

'Two days! Antonio—'

'I've already lost three months, Maisie. What's really holding you here, besides an aversion to falling in with my plans?'

'Lots of things!'

'Name one, then.'

She stared at him, infuriated that he would reduce her life to a list that could be ticked off and discarded. 'I have friends, you know.'

He shrugged. 'I'm sure you do. But I also imagine that they are friends from school, and you don't see them very often.'

Maisie bit her lip, not wanting to admit how close to the truth that was. Besides her old college friends, she'd made a few friends through a local baby group, but the relationships were new and she could hardly claim they were worth staying for.

'And what about Max?' she countered, because her brother was of course the biggest reason for her to stay. 'How could I leave him?' She could hardly imagine it.

Antonio stared at her levelly for a full minute, the look in his piercing blue eyes turning strangely gentle, which made Maisie even more nervous. She felt nervous just *looking* at him, as if she was approaching a magnetic force field, about to be sucked in. She'd never met such a compelling man before, never felt that relentless and exciting tug inside her as she had with Antonio, and it was all magnified when he was looking at her with such kindness.

'What?' she demanded, her voice coming out in little more than a squeak.

'Don't you think,' Antonio said, 'it might be better for Max if you came with me to Milan?'

Maisie jerked back as if he'd slapped her, and Ella stirred against her breast, opening her eyes to gaze up at her mother in sleepy frustration. She screwed her face up, about to let out a howl of protest, and Maisie quickly soothed her, bending her head so Antonio couldn't see the expression on her face. How hurt she was. How afraid she was that he might be right.

'What do you mean by that?' she asked in a low voice when Ella had settled again, although she wasn't sure she really wanted to know.

'Only that Max is twenty-three years old, a single man in the city with a steady job and good prospects. He's given up a lot to support you, just as you gave up so much to do the same for him.'

Maisie stared down at Ella miserably, a lump forming in her throat. She knew Antonio was right, and she hated it.

'You don't want him to sacrifice so many years the way

you did, Maisie, do you?' His voice was so very gentle. 'You want more for him than that. That's why you made the sacrifice in the first place.'

How could a man whose professional reputation as a ruthless destroyer of businesses and people's lives have so much compassionate perception? It seemed unfair somehow.

'There's a difference between giving Max a bit of space and moving halfway across the world,' Maisie finally said, the words feeling as if they had to be dragged from her.

'Perhaps,' Antonio acknowledged, 'but only one of those options would truly give Max his freedom. He wouldn't agree to give you the space you both need unless he was sure you were cared for. You know that.'

Maisie flinched and looked away. Yes, she did know that. But did that really mean moving to Milan with Antonio? With every word he spoke she felt the walls closing in. She didn't want to move to Milan…and it had nothing to do with Max, or her friends, or her life in New York. It had to do with the man in front of her, a man who affected her now as much as he had a year ago. A man who would hold her life and her happiness in his hands, and it was that prospect that terrified her.

Antonio watched the emotions play across Maisie's lovely, open face. She couldn't hide anything—not her fear, her misery, or the realisation that he was right. He felt sorry for her, but he also felt a surge of satisfaction and triumph. She was going to agree. It was simply a matter of time.

'So I'm doing this for Max,' Maisie said in a shaky voice. 'And you. And Ella.'

'And you,' Antonio said swiftly. 'This doesn't need to be a sacrifice, Maisie. Heaven knows you've made enough of those in your life.'

'Right.' Her lips trembled and she looked away, out at the azure sky and bright lemon-yellow sun sparkling over Manhattan's midtown. Ella stirred again, her eyes opening, showing them to be a piercing, vivid blue, just like his. *His daughter.* The realisation hit him afresh yet again, making his heart tumble in his chest. He didn't have space or time to feel sorry for Maisie. Not now, when his daughter's life was at stake. His life.

'You could have a better life in Milan, you know, if you wanted to.'

She turned to him, her green eyes wide. 'How?'

'You'll have better living accommodation, certainly,' Antonio said. 'And there might be more opportunities for music, who knows? Without having to worry about money, you could be free to pursue your own studies or ambitions.'

'So,' Maisie answered slowly, 'you're willing to pay child support if I do as you say and move to Milan, but not if I stay here in my home?' Her eyes flashed and her lips trembled before she pressed them together. 'That doesn't seem exactly fair, Antonio. It feels like blackmail.'

'And does it seem fair that I pay for you and Ella and never get to see her?' Antonio countered, quashing the flicker of guilt Maisie's words had caused to ripple through him. Was he strong-arming her into this? Why couldn't she just see *sense*? 'There has to be some compromise.'

'I don't see much compromise with me moving to where you are,' Maisie snapped.

'What's really keeping you here, Maisie?' Antonio tried to gentle his tone. Riding roughshod over her feelings wasn't going to accomplish his goal, and right now all he wanted, all he needed, was for Maisie to agree to move to Italy. Then he could see Ella; he could maintain control and order and distance in a way that satisfied them both.

'If it's Max, I've already said he needs his freedom. But I'll be happy to fly him to Milan to visit as many times as you both want.'

Maisie rocked Ella as she shook her head. 'It's not just Max.'

'Then what?' Antonio demanded.

'Everything, Antonio,' she cried. 'You're asking me to put my life, and my daughter's life, in your hands. And, while you might be Ella's father, you're still a stranger to me. I can't help but be more than a little nervous about dropping my entire life to follow you to a foreign country where I don't know anyone.' Her eyes flashed. 'I think I'm a pretty strong person. After my parents died, and we found out there was no money, I soldiered on. I made a home for my brother and me, and I saw him through college. And when I found out I was pregnant I did the same thing. I made it work. But that doesn't mean I want to walk into a difficult or even impossible situation, one I know little to nothing about, with someone I can't...'

'Can't...?' Antonio repeated dangerously.

'Can't trust,' she said, a mutinous tilt to her chin. 'Yet.'

Antonio let out a slow, even breath, determined not to be hurt by her honesty. 'Fair enough,' he said. 'I accept we don't know each other very well. So I'll put safeguards in place. You can own the house you live in outright, and have a monthly allowance that won't change, no matter what, on direct debit. I'll put it all in writing so you can be completely reassured.'

Maisie stared at him, her expression both stunned and stricken. 'That's...that's very generous, Antonio, but it's not just about money.'

He stared at her, nonplussed. 'Then what is it about?'

'My life,' she cried. 'And Ella's life. What if—if Ella gets attached to you and then after a few months or years you feel you've had enough? You want to go back to your bimbos and business dismantling?' Her expression turned fierce, her eyes glittering. 'I won't let you break her heart.'

For a second Antonio had the bizarre sensation that Maisie hadn't just been talking about their daughter. But that was, of course, nonsense. She didn't like him. She'd made that plain, and it was probably easier if she continued in the same vein. 'You clearly have a very low opinion of me,' he remarked, keeping his voice toneless.

'I need to be careful. For Ella's sake.'

'Let's at least agree on a trial period, then,' Antonio suggested. 'Six months. If you're not satisfied I'm in it for the long haul at the end of six months, we can renegotiate. But you have to agree to stay in Milan for that time.'

He held her gaze, willing her to agree, even as a bitter little seed of fear inside him hoped she wouldn't. That little seed made him long to run away from this—from Maisie, from Ella—because who was he to attempt to be a father? Have a family? His examples of both were appalling, and the blood-red stain of guilt would always be on his soul. But Maisie didn't need to know any of that.

'Six months,' she said slowly, turning the words over. Antonio nodded.

'Six months.'

She held his gaze, and the air seemed to tauten and shimmer between them. She looked like Botticelli's Venus, with her curly red-gold hair surrounding her lovely, heart-shaped face, her eyes wide and vivid green, her pink lips slightly parted. In her arms Ella gurgled and cooed, and the simple sound of innocence tightened something inside Antonio, nearly making him snap. He wanted this. He'd lost so much in his life, messed it up, given it away, but he wanted this. He needed it.

Maisie broke their locked gazes first, her lashes fanning her cheeks as she looked downwards. 'All right,' she whispered, and Antonio felt a clench of triumph, a spasm of fear. He wanted this…but what if he failed yet again? What if he lost it all? He didn't think he had it in him to pay for his sins a second time.

CHAPTER NINE

MAISIE STARED OUT at the cloudless blue sky as the jet took off from the tarmac, her stomach dropping with both the motion and the enormity of what she was doing. Had already done.

The last two days had been a blur of activity as she'd prepared to leave her life in New York and move to Milan. Max had been both incredulous and worried, but even amidst his protestations that she couldn't go running off with a virtual stranger, never mind that he was Ella's father, Maisie had detected the tiniest flicker of relief in his eyes. The protests had died off with surprising speed, and instead he'd helped her pack.

But more than for Max, Maisie had to believe she was doing the right thing for Ella. Antonio *was* Ella's father, and he deserved the chance to have a relationship with his daughter. And it was only for six months. Although right now, watching from the window as the plane soared up into the sky, six months felt like a very long time.

The motion of the plane had sent Ella to sleep, but now as it levelled out she stirred, opening wide blue eyes to look around in curiosity. Maisie glanced at Antonio, who had been looking at something on his tablet since they'd taken off. In fact, in the two days since she'd made the decision to come to Milan he'd become steadily more and more remote, making Maisie question her decision before she'd even put it into action. It was as if Antonio had got what he wanted, and was done with her…and with Ella.

He hadn't even held his daughter yet, or looked at her properly. It made Maisie wonder, with more than a touch of panic, why he wanted the two of them to come to Italy with him. Was he going to be like this for ever?

'Antonio?' she asked quietly, and he glanced up from his tablet, eyes narrowing.

'Yes?'

Maisie steeled herself against that look. Why did she feel as if she was a burden to him already? Taking up his precious time? This was exactly what she had been afraid of, in the dark corners of her mind and heart. That by coming to Italy, by trusting herself to him even in just the practical matters, she'd start to feel useless. Burdensome. Adrift.

Her life in New York might not have seemed like much to a man like him, but it had been hers and she'd worked hard for it. The last thing she wanted was to feel like an irritation on the periphery of someone's life.

'Maisie?' Antonio prompted, a touch of impatience in his voice.

'Would you like to hold Ella?' Maisie asked. 'You haven't held her yet. You've barely looked at her.' She hadn't meant to sound accusing, but she saw Antonio flinch. Maisie took a slow, even breath. 'All I meant,' she said carefully, 'is that you've said you want to get to know her. We have an eight-hour flight ahead of us, and surely there's no time like the present?'

Antonio glanced at Ella, his face full of a sudden, surprising uncertainty. 'I've never held a baby before.'

Was he actually *nervous*? 'It's like falling off a log.'

He gave her the glimmer of a smile. 'Somehow I doubt that.'

'Still.'

Antonio glanced again at Ella, as if studying a problem and thinking how best to solve it. 'How do you do it?'

'Supporting the head is the most important thing, although not as crucial as when she was a newborn. She's stronger and sturdier now. She won't break.' Gently Maisie hoisted Ella up and held her out. 'Try?'

Antonio drew back. 'I don't…'

'Please, Antonio.' And then, because she thought he needed the encouragement, she added softly, 'You can do this.'

Something flickered across Antonio's face and then he held out his arms, awkwardly. Maisie handed Ella to him.

The sight of their daughter in Antonio's arms felt strangely, surprisingly profound. Antonio cradled her easily, her head resting in the crook of his elbow as she blinked up at him with wide blue eyes so like his own.

A small, incredulous smile tugged the corner of his mouth. 'Well, hello there, *bella*,' he said softly. *'Ciao.'*

Maisie let out a little laugh, a sound of pure emotion. She felt, bizarrely, near tears. 'You'll have to teach her Italian.'

'Yes,' Antonio answered, sounding firm, even fervent. 'I will.'

'And me, as well.' Too late Maisie realised they weren't likely to have that kind of relationship. Although Antonio hadn't laid out the specifics, she'd gathered enough from what he'd said that they would live separate lives in Milan, connected only by their daughter.

'Yes,' Antonio said after a second's pause, shooting her a swift, searching glance. 'And you.'

'I can just get a tutor,' she half mumbled. 'Or do something online…'

'Why do something online when you have someone to

teach you in person?' Antonio countered. He turned back to Ella, his whole countenance softening. Ella blinked up at him, looking serious in a way only babies could look, and then, quite suddenly, a smile burst across her face like a rainbow, and she let out a gurgle, the sound one of pure joy.

Antonio blinked, seeming stunned, and then an answering smile bloomed across his face and he pressed a kiss to his daughter's forehead.

Maisie looked away, blinking back tears. She hadn't expected to be so emotionally affected by the sight of Antonio with Ella. His daughter. Their daughter. For better or worse they were a family. The doubts that had been plaguing her mind like a flock of black crows started to disperse. It was the right decision to come to Milan. And maybe, just maybe, it would all work out well. If she worked at it. If they both did.

A few minutes later Ella started to fuss, and Maisie took her back from Antonio for a feed.

'That's something I can't do,' he remarked wryly, and Maisie blushed, feeling exposed despite the blanket draped across her shoulder, hiding Ella and her unbuttoned shirt from view. This all felt so strange and intimate, and yet weirdly right too. It made everything inside her feel jangled and mixed up.

'So tell me about Milan,' she said as Ella relaxed against her. 'I've never been to Europe or anywhere, really.'

'Where did you grow up?'

'Upstate New York. I only moved to the city for school.'

'And Max?'

'He went to Cornell, and lived at home to save money. When he got the internship in the city, it seemed meant to be.' She smiled, the curve of her lips touched with sadness.

'But I know you were right. He needs his freedom. It's good for him that I'm going, even if it's only for six months.'

Antonio's dark, straight brows drew together. 'I hope it's not only for six months.'

'Trial period, remember?' Maisie tried to speak lightly.

'Yes, but I fully intend for that trial to be a success.'

'How is it meant to work exactly, Antonio?' Maisie bit her lip. She hadn't meant to get serious so soon; she'd started this conversation intending for Antonio to tell her about the tourist sights. But perhaps it was better this way, because she needed to know.

'I suppose we'll make it up as we go along,' Antonio said slowly. 'I'm new to this too, obviously. The first thing is to get you and Ella settled. I've already arranged for us to view some suitable houses tomorrow.'

'So soon?'

'The sooner you both feel at home, the better.'

Or the sooner he could get them out of his own house and life? Maisie couldn't escape the feeling that Antonio was trying to put her and Ella into a tidy little compartment and keep them there. It shouldn't bother her really, because she didn't want to become emotionally attached to Antonio. That would be disastrous…for both her and Ella. It was the thing she was most afraid of.

After Ella had dozed off, the flight attendant kindly provided a bassinet for her to sleep in.

'It takes a steady hand,' Antonio murmured as Maisie performed the tricky manoeuvre of getting Ella into the cot without waking her up. She held her breath as her daughter stirred, her face screwing up as if she were about to let out a blood-curdling scream before she suddenly relaxed, eyelids fluttering, and let out a breathy sigh of sleep.

Maisie matched it with her own sigh of relief as she sank back into her seat. 'Hopefully she'll sleep for a few hours at least.' She glanced out at the darkening sky. 'It's already past her bedtime.'

'You said she has trouble sleeping?'

'No more than most babies.' For some reason Maisie felt defensive, as if Antonio was questioning whether she was a good mother. 'She's barely three months old. She'll settle down into a routine, I'm sure.'

'I'm sure.'

Maisie glanced out of the window, the sky darkening to indigo. Their lounger seats in First Class felt like a secluded and private enclave, even more so now that Ella was asleep. Alone with Antonio, without her baby to focus on and use as a sort of barrier, Maisie didn't know how to act with this man who was still more stranger than not. Didn't know how to feel.

A flight attendant paused by their seats to give them menus. Maisie glanced down at the options for a five-course meal, bemused.

'This sounds better than anything I've ever eaten in a restaurant,' she remarked.

'It certainly beats Economy Class,' Antonio answered with a smile.

Maisie laughed and shook her head. 'I wouldn't know. I've never even been on an airplane.' Antonio looked so surprised that she half wished she hadn't admitted as much. It seemed she was always going to be acknowledging her innocence, her inexperience. She knew nothing of life because the years she should have been at school, exploring the city and learning about life, she'd been working two full-time jobs to support her and Max. Right now it made her feel terribly gauche.

'I look forward to introducing you to some new experiences, then,' Antonio said smoothly, and Maisie couldn't decide if there was innuendo, or even intent, in his tone.

He'd introduced her to some rather extraordinary new experiences already. 'But first,' Antonio added, nodding towards her menu, 'let's order.'

Antonio watched Maisie eye him uncertainly and wondered what he was playing at. No doubt she was wondering, too. Somehow, thousands of miles up in the air, it felt easy to discard his rules and resolutions and simply *be,* enjoying time spent with both Maisie and Ella. Flirt a little even.

Holding his daughter had been an extraordinary experience. He'd been wary of it, because when it came to family relationships he feared he was the opposite of Midas, with everything he touched turning to ruin. But then Maisie had handed Ella to him, and he'd had no choice but to take her. It had been the most wonderful thing in the world; her smile had reached right inside him and grabbed his heart. Squeezed hard, and never let go. Now more than ever he knew he'd made the right decision in bringing Maisie and Ella to Italy with him. No matter what.

As for Maisie… Antonio couldn't come up with an acceptable explanation for ordering champagne with their dinner, or clinking glasses, or giving her a slow, considering smile as they sipped fizz and worked their way through five courses while Ella slept and the lights in the first-class cabin darkened, making everything feel more intimate. No reason at all…and yet he did it. Because he wanted to.

As they ate and drank he asked about her childhood, what life was like when her parents were alive, how she had got into music and what she liked most about performing. The questions came naturally, seeming to surprise them both. Maisie's answers started out stumbling and uncertain, but gradually became more confident and interested.

'I love playing the violin, but it's a private thing,' she said as he poured more champagne and they started on their main course. 'Performing has never interested me as much. The music itself is what feeds my soul, not whether people are listening.'

'Feeds your soul,' Antonio repeated musingly. 'An interesting turn of phrase.'

'What feeds your soul, Antonio?' Maisie asked lightly. 'Taking apart companies?' He glanced at her appraisingly, acknowledging the very slightly scornful note in her voice.

'Sorry.' She grimaced. 'I shouldn't have said that. I don't mean to spoil the mood…'

'But you don't agree with what I do.' He stated it mildly, or tried to.

'No, I don't.' She lifted her chin in a gesture Antonio already recognised as the way she gathered her courage. 'Ruining people's lives, all for the sake of profit…'

'They were going to be ruined anyway.' He tried to keep his voice even, tried not to feel the hurt. What did he care if Maisie thought he was some ruthless, renegade businessman? The newspapers and gossip rags liked to paint that picture, and he kept the altruistic side of his business ventures quiet. Very quiet. In any case, having Maisie think he was some cruel businessman was better than her knowing the truth.

'Were they really going to be ruined?' she asked, angling her chin a fraction higher. 'Or would some jobs be saved, some *lives* be saved, if the companies didn't want to maximise their profit?'

'The companies I work with are already being taken over.' Antonio hadn't wanted to justify himself, and yet he knew that was exactly what he was doing. He was nettled that Maisie had assumed the worst about him, even though he knew it was better that she did. He would only disappoint her otherwise. 'They bring me in to try to minimise the damage, not maximise it.'

'Then why do the newspapers say you're so ruthless?'

'I *can* be ruthless,' he admitted. 'Takeovers are by their very nature ruthless. People lose jobs. Lives are ruined. And that sells more newspapers than any good I might have been able to do.'

Maisie's lips twisted. 'It just seems such a…sordid line of work.'

'Someone's got to do it.'

'But you're really in property, aren't you? Buying and selling?'

'Yes.'

'And that building you knocked down…?'

He sighed. 'It was a disaster waiting to happen, Maisie.'

He didn't like having this conversation, even as he acknowledged it was better that they have a little distance between them. He couldn't let the champagne and dim lighting lull him into wanting something that was impossible.

'Maybe we should talk about something else,' Maisie suggested, and Antonio gave a terse nod. Damn it, why was he feeling so *hurt?*

'I asked you about Milan,' she reminded him gently. 'What sights are there to see?'

Dutifully Antonio listed some of the museums and parks in the city, as well as the fantastic shopping. Maisie listened attentively, her eyes alight with interest.

'Perhaps one weekend we can go to one of the lakes,' he found himself suggesting. 'They're not too far away and they are very beautiful.'

'That would be wonderful,' Maisie said, and he saw that flicker of uncertainty in her eyes that he'd seen before, and felt in himself. Images of the two of them on a picnic blanket, Ella lying between them and the lake sparkling in the spring sunshine, flitted through his mind. Happy families, but that wasn't what was going on here. It couldn't be, because what did he know about happy families? He only knew how to destroy them. Maisie had been right when she'd called him the ruthless destroyer, but she had no idea…and Antonio wasn't going to enlighten her. He'd told her enough on that one regrettable and wonderful night.

'It's getting late,' he said, his voice a little rough. 'We should sleep.'

Maisie nodded, and they both settled down into the comfortable seats that extended nearly horizontally to form a bed. As tired as he was, too many thoughts and feelings were flying around in his head for him to settle. A deep and primal satisfaction that he had Maisie and Ella with him warred with a creeping unease and fear that he was doing the wrong thing. A dangerous thing…for all three of them.

As sleep started to invade the fringes of his mind, his guard relaxed and he fell into one of his old, torturous dreams. Paolo was glaring at him, his hands clenched into fists at his sides.

Why did you let me? You should have known better.

Of course, Paolo had never said those words. He'd never had the chance. But his mother and father had both said them, before they'd stopped speaking to Antonio completely. Before he'd destroyed his own family.

I'm sorry, Paolo. So sorry.

In the dream Antonio never seemed to be able to get the words out; they crowded in his mouth like marbles and he choked on them. Because words meant nothing. They certainly weren't enough, and they didn't make a difference now. Paolo was dead, and it was entirely Antonio's fault.

'Antonio… Antonio!' A soft hand gently shook his shoulder, and Antonio blinked up into Maisie's concerned face. 'You were thrashing about in your sleep… Are you okay?'

Thrashing about? He jerked up to a sitting position, running his hand through his hair as he took a slow, steadying breath. 'I'm fine.'

'You didn't seem fine,' Maisie said quietly. 'Was it a bad dream?'

She made him sound like a child. Antonio shook his head, irritable now, because that was better than being desperate. 'I'm *fine*.'

Ella let out a startled cry, and he grimaced. He must have woken her up with his angry tone. Maisie reached for her. 'She's probably hungry again. I'll feed her.'

Antonio nodded, trying to get his flayed emotions back under wraps as Maisie nursed their baby, a blanket draped over her shoulder. Even after a feed Ella wouldn't settle, and Maisie threw Antonio an exasperated look. 'She's fretful at night sometimes.'

'Why don't I walk her up and down the plane? You said movement helped.'

Maisie looked surprised. 'Only if you want to…'

'Of course I want to.' Antonio took Ella, cradling her in his arms, amazed at the soft, sleepy feel of her. She nestled into him, and his heart swelled with both love and fear. She was so very precious.

Maisie watched them, her expression softening, and Antonio gave her a quick smile. 'We'll be fine.' He hoped.

He strolled up and down the aisle, bouncing her gently and humming under his breath—one of the lullabies from his childhood. Eventually Ella stopped squirming and squawking and Antonio watched as her eyes shut, her breath coming out in milky sighs. He stroked her downy hair, her head fitting perfectly into his palm. She was tiny and fragile and beautiful, and already he loved her. Already he knew he would do anything for her, sacrifice everything for her safety and happiness. The feeling was deep, instinctive, and overwhelming.

This time he wouldn't mess up. He wouldn't ruin everything. This time he would get it right, for Ella's sake as well as his own.

CHAPTER TEN

'WHAT DO YOU THINK?'

Maisie gazed around the yawning foyer of the enormous villa on the outskirts of Milan, overwhelmed by the sheer grandiose luxury of the place.

'It's huge.'

Antonio flicked a glance at the brochure. 'Four thousand square feet. Hardly enormous.'

'Maybe not by your standards.' She jiggled Ella against her chest as she walked around the marble-paved hall, a double staircase leading to a balcony above. As they'd driven up, she'd seen that the circular driveway had a huge, ornate fountain. The place was a palace. 'I don't mean to sound ungrateful, but I'd feel like I was swimming in a place like this. Couldn't we look at somewhere…smaller?'

'You want somewhere smaller?' Antonio sounded disbelieving.

'Yes. Cosier.'

'Very well.' Antonio glanced at the realtor who was standing by the door. 'Roberto?'

'Bene, bene.' Roberto smiled at them both. 'I have such places. Small, but perfect.'

Feeling guilty for not liking a place that was so opulent and enormous, Maisie followed them back out to the waiting limo. They'd arrived in Milan yesterday afternoon and started house-hunting today. Her head was still spinning, and not just with jet lag.

She couldn't figure Antonio out. One moment he was wining and dining her in First Class; the next he was shutting himself off, seemingly deliberately, everything about him closed and cold. He was gentle and loving with Ella, and then he blanked Maisie. She felt exhausted simply trying to decipher his moods and the reasons for them. And, worst of all, every time he acted cool or remote she started to doubt whether she should have come to Milan at all. Whether she could survive the emotional roller coaster Antonio put her on just by existing.

Because the truth was, she cared for him in some small way. When she saw him with Ella, when he asked her about herself, she remembered the gentle and passionate and hurting man she'd met on that night nearly a year ago. She remembered him and wanted him, even if he wasn't real—at least, not the real Antonio. The trouble was, wanting that man was a very dangerous and foolish thing to do.

They'd barely spoken beyond the basics since they'd arrived in Italy; Maisie had been exhausted and Ella fretful, and she'd fallen asleep in a huge king-sized bed in the guest room of Antonio's apartment, on the top floor of an elegant *palazzo* in the historic city centre.

She'd woken to find Antonio immersed in his laptop, and she'd explored the apartment, only to realise it was the ultimate bachelor pad, from the media room to the rooftop gym, to the sleek, clearly unused kitchen. The surfaces were all hard, marble or steel, the furniture angular and uncompromising, the spiral staircase a stunning centrepiece as well as a death trap for a baby who would be crawling in a few months. The sooner she found her own place the better, and not just because of the silly stairs.

Twenty-four hours into her sojourn in Italy, and Maisie

realised how important it was going to be to make her own life…away from Antonio, his changeable moods and her own dangerous desires.

She glanced at him now, his sharply angled jaw freshly shaven, his piercing blue eyes narrowed as he focused on the screen of his phone. He was dressed in an expertly tailored business suit of steel-grey. He looked devastatingly attractive, and as remote as ever. Maisie looked at him and her mind emptied out. Her heart started to pound. It was ridiculous.

She turned back to Ella, pointing out cars and trees along the road, trying to distract herself in meaningless babble.

Fifteen minutes later they pulled up to a far more modest yet still elegant house in a village on the outskirts of Milan. Maisie immediately liked the friendly-looking house, with its bright red shutters and wrought-iron railing trailing bougainvillea. Inside, dark wood beams crisscrossed a whitewashed ceiling; there was a living room with squashy sofas and a deep stone fireplace, and the dining room led into the open-plan kitchen, with French windows overlooking a terrace and garden, complete with a fenced-in pool. Upstairs there were three bedrooms—a master with a sumptuous en-suite bathroom, and two smaller bedrooms. Maisie stood in the last bedroom, by a stone-silled window overlooking the garden.

'Is that a fig tree?' she asked as Antonio came into the room.

'It looks like it.'

'This is perfect.' She turned to him with a smile, Ella in her arms. 'Cosy and friendly. It's not too much?' She still felt uncomfortable with the prospect of him paying for everything, but she didn't have much choice. Besides, he had asked, or rather demanded, that she come here.

'Too much?' His eyebrows rose. 'It's a positive bargain,

considering the other places I was thinking of. And fortunately it is available immediately.'

'Great.' She tried to keep her voice upbeat, battling a mixture of elation and fear. It would be lovely to have her own house, but she was being plopped in a small village in a foreign country, without speaking a word of the language. It was a little daunting, to say the least.

'Obviously you will need some baby items here,' Antonio continued. 'If you make a list, I will make sure they arrive by this evening.'

'This evening?' She shook her head in amazement. 'Do you have a magic wand?'

'No, just a magic chequebook.' He flashed her a brief smile that didn't reach his eyes. 'Just let me know what you need.'

The next few hours were a blur of activity as they returned to Antonio's apartment and packed up her and Ella's things. She gave him her list, instinctively trying to keep the number of items down, but Antonio barely looked at it before pocketing it.

'Let me know if you need anything else,' he said. He'd given her a top-of-the-line smartphone and entered several numbers into its contacts—his office, his private line, his mobile. Despite the phone numbers, she didn't feel he was particularly accessible, at least not in the way she wanted.

And so, just a few hours after seeing the pretty villa, Maisie found herself standing in her new home, Ella in her arms, her suitcases by her feet as Antonio's driver closed the door on her. Home sweet home. Here she was.

Taking a deep breath, she told herself not to feel lonely or uncertain or afraid—basically all the things she was feeling—and to start making the villa feel like home.

After feeding Ella, she put her down for a nap on the

king-sized bed, surrounded by pillows. Thankfully Ella couldn't roll over yet, and so Maisie was sure she'd be safe.

While her daughter slept, she unpacked her belongings—two suitcases and her violin was all she had, so it didn't take long. She pottered about in the kitchen and explored the garden, the air warm and dry, scented with flowers, the sun shining high above. Really, this was paradise. Right now, though, it was a bit lonely in paradise.

When Ella woke up, Maisie took her out to the garden, laying her on a blanket underneath the fig tree she'd seen earlier from the window. She tilted her head up to the sun and closed her eyes as Ella gurgled beside her. Slowly, she felt herself start to relax. Life here could be good.

Perhaps later she would put Ella in her stroller and explore the village, find out if there were any baby groups to join. She'd make friends; she'd figure out a way. She just had no idea what part, whether small or large, Antonio would play in her life...or what part she wanted him to have.

The sound of a car pulling up in front of the villa had Maisie springing up from the blanket. Had Antonio come back? Why did that thought make her feel so hopeful, so excited?

But it wasn't Antonio; it was a delivery man bringing in package after package, the items arriving mere hours after she'd given Antonio the list.

Maisie laid Ella on a blanket in the living room while she began to open the parcels and packages. It felt better than Christmas, a feast for the senses, as she opened a top-of-the-range cot along with pink flannel sheets and an embroidered duvet, a high chair, a bouncy chair, a car seat, a musical mobile and a whole host of toys, blankets and other baby accessories. Maisie felt overwhelmed.

Ella was starting to fuss so she decided to leave all the

toys and equipment and go for a walk. She hoped the village had a shop, because the house was empty of any food.

The day was still warm even though it was late afternoon, and with Ella in her stroller Maisie spent a happy hour wandering the ancient, narrow streets of the little village. She happened upon a tiny shop that sold all sorts of delicious food and stocked up on mozzarella, tomatoes and basil, enjoying the scent and texture of the fresh fruits and vegetables and doing her best to mime her needs to the smiling, apple-cheeked woman behind the till. By the time she started back, Ella was ready for her next feed and the sky was starting to turn violet at the edges.

'Where have you been?'

The ringing, accusatory tone had Maisie freezing as she turned up the drive of the villa. Antonio stood by the front door, a chauffeur-driven limo parked in front. He looked thunderous and far too attractive, having shed his suit jacket, loosened his tie and rolled up the sleeves of his crisp white shirt. Everything about him radiated power and authority as well as blatant sex appeal.

'I went out for a walk,' Maisie said, striving to sound cool rather than apologetic. 'I didn't realise I had to tell you all my movements.'

'I've been waiting here for the better part of an hour. You didn't think to take your phone?'

'I didn't realise it was meant to be a tracking device.' Maisie slipped by Antonio and unlocked the front door as he dismissed his driver. She unbuckled Ella from her stroller and went inside. 'She needs to be fed,' she said shortly. Antonio watched, still looking annoyed, as Maisie settled herself in one of the squashy armchairs in the living room and started to feed Ella. She could feel the tension and anger simmering in him, and didn't fully understand it. Did he expect her to be at his beck and call? Was that how this was going to be?

'Why did you come by, anyway?' she asked, and realised belatedly how ungracious she sounded, especially after all the things Antonio had arranged to be sent to the villa.

'To see my daughter,' Antonio said, his voice as short as hers had been. 'And to help put the cot together.'

'Oh.' Now she felt guilty for being so hostile, but why had *he* been so hostile? 'Thank you,' she said after a pause. 'But Antonio, I have to confess that you confuse me. At times you seem so kind and interested, and at other times…' She gestured to the space between them, helpless to explain. 'If this has any chance of working, we need to establish some kind of system or ground rules. A way to get along without everything turning into a battle. Otherwise I think I might go a little bit crazy.'

Antonio stared at Maisie, her expression one of open, sympathetic appeal, and tried to suppress the guilt and irritation coursing through him. The truth was, he hadn't had a good reason to show up only hours after Maisie had settled into her new home, except that he knew he wanted to see her as well as Ella.

But instead of the happy, cheerful scene he'd envisioned of his putting together the cot and maybe even staying for supper, everything had turned to tension and hostility and suspicion. Why should he even be surprised?

'You've ruined this family, Antonio.'

Even now he could see his mother's grief-ravaged face and felt the familiar twist in his gut. But that was in the past, and this—Ella—was his future. He couldn't give up on her. He wouldn't.

'I'm sorry,' he said finally. 'I don't mean to be confusing. This is new for me, Maisie, just as it is for you. I've never...' He paused, sifting through his words as well as his emotions. 'I've never had a child before obviously, but neither have I had a serious relationship of any kind.' He shrugged. 'You know my history nearly as well as I do, I suspect.'

Maisie gave a little grimace. 'Only from those unfortunate tabloids.'

'Well, then,' he said lightly. 'Don't believe everything you read, but believe some of it.'

'The general gist?'

'Yes.'

'So why are you here, then, Antonio? If you really are the reckless, careless playboy those magazines make you out to be, why do you care so much about your daughter?'

He flinched at her bluntness, even as he acknowledged she had a point. 'My own family was a bit of a mess,' he said, choosing each word with care. 'And part of that, a large part, was my fault. I want to get it right this time.'

'How was it your fault?' She frowned. 'You said something similar that night...'

'There's no point talking about what's in the past.' The last thing he needed was a reminder of all the weakness and vulnerability he'd spewed forth that night. He'd been drunk and desperate and pathetic. He didn't want to live it all over again. 'And I admit, I've been surprised by the strength of my feelings. I never thought I'd have children, but now that my daughter's right here...' He gestured to Ella nursing happily. 'I love her,' he said simply. 'I want to do my best by her. I might not get a lot of the other stuff right, but I will try with Ella, I swear.'

'I believe you,' Maisie said softly. She sounded sad. 'Why don't you have a look at the cot? It would be great if she could sleep in it tonight.'

Antonio nodded, accepting her suggestion as the dismissal he suspected it was. Better for the both of them, really. No need to spill secrets, or get close. No need at all.

He spent the next hour squinting at the complicated directions for the cot, finally managing to put it together as darkness settled softly outside, over the fig tree.

From downstairs he heard the sounds of Maisie moving around, and then some cooking smells—frying pancetta and garlic—that made his mouth water.

With the cot assembled, he made it up with the new sheets and quilt, attached the mobile up above and snuggled a few soft toys in the corners. Then he went downstairs in search of Maisie and Ella.

The scene that greeted him was so warm and welcoming he nearly felt his eyes sting. Ella was waving her chubby legs in the air as she lay on a blanket in the living room, in sight of Maisie in the kitchen, who was stirring a pan of something that smelled delicious. The table was set for two, surprising him.

Maisie turned to him with a small smile, a hint of uncertainty lurking in her eyes along with the welcome. 'It's so late… I thought you might want to stay for dinner. That is, if you don't have any other plans.'

He didn't have any plans. He'd been hoping for this very scenario, and yet…still he hesitated. Longing and fear battled against each other, alarm bell ringing. They were meant to keep a certain distance, relate only through their daughter. But they had to get along. And he was hungry.

'Sure,' he said with a smile and a shrug. 'Thank you.' Maisie smiled back and Antonio tried not to notice the way it lit her eyes up like emerald stars, or the way the light caught the gold hints in her hair, or the curve of her breast and hip underneath the loose T-shirt she wore. Or, he acknowledged grimly as he shifted where he stood, the memory of how those warm, generous curves had felt against his palms and lips.

'I even splurged and bought a bottle of wine,' Maisie said as she nodded towards a bottle of red on the counter top. 'I don't usually drink, but since this is Italy…'

'When in Rome…' Antonio murmured. He retrieved a corkscrew from the drawer, opening the bottle and pouring them both a glass.

'You're corrupting me, you know,' Maisie teased. 'Whisky and then champagne and now wine…' Antonio froze, and she frowned. 'What is it?'

'Nothing.' He wasn't about to explain what a good, or awful, corrupter of innocence he was. How his mother had accused him of the same thing, used virtually the same words, and it had had nothing to do with something as innocuous as a glass of champagne or a bottle of wine.

You corrupted him, Antonio. You ruined him.

'I feel like I said something wrong.' She gazed at him seriously. 'I was just joking, you know.'

'I know.'

She looked as if she wanted to say something more but Antonio forestalled her by handing her a glass of wine. 'Drink up.'

'I should only have a little, since I'm breastfeeding.' She took a sip, smiling at him. 'Thank you for all this. The cot, the toys, everything.'

'It's all ready upstairs for Ella. Do you want to see?' He found he was rather looking forward to her seeing the room and the work that he'd done.

'Yes, I do.' She scooped up Ella. 'Why don't you show me now? The pasta won't be ready for another few minutes.'

He led the way up the stairs and then down the darkened corridor, flicking on a table lamp so the nursery was bathed in a cosy glow.

'Oh, Antonio…it looks amazing.' She stroked one hand over the quilt embroidered with lambs and ducks, and then touched the fleecy bunny tucked into one corner. 'It's perfect. Thank you.' She laid Ella down in the cot, and the baby smiled as she blinked up at the spinning mobile.

'And one more thing.' He reached above her head to pull the string on the mobile, and a violin rendition of a Brahms lullaby began to play.

'Oh…' Tears sparkled in Maisie's eyes as she listened to the soothing strains.

'Perhaps you'll play it to her yourself one day.'

'That's so thoughtful of you, Antonio. Really.' She laid a hand on his arm, and just like that the tender feeling between them sparked into something else. Something hot and dangerous.

Her fingers flexed on his arm and Antonio drew a shuddering breath. The very air seemed to crackle between them, and his gaze fell to her parted lips as his body remembered the honeyed taste of them and longed to experience it again.

Maisie shifted towards him, her head angled so that it would be all too easy to close the small space between their mouths and swallow it up. Antonio didn't think she even realised what she was doing, how open the invitation was…or how much he wanted to accept it.

Then Ella let out a little cry, and the effect of that single sound was as if a vat of iced water had been poured onto both of them. Maisie jumped a little and Antonio straightened, raking a hand through his hair. That had been a close call. Far, far too close.

'The pasta is probably ready…'

'I'll take Ella.' Maisie hurried out of the room while Antonio scooped up his daughter and breathed in her baby scent. What madness had possessed him just then? He couldn't get involved with Maisie again. He couldn't let her get close. He knew where that led, and it was nowhere good. She already knew too much about him. What would happen when she knew the full, terrible truth?

Slowly Antonio walked down the stairs. He set Ella back on her blanket as Maisie dished out the pasta onto two plates. Everything about the scene was warm, welcoming, and lovely.

Antonio stepped towards the door. At the sound of his footsteps, Maisie turned.

'Antonio...?' A frown crinkled her forehead.

'I'm sorry, but I can't stay after all.' The words were terse, too terse. He saw hurt flash across Maisie's face before she steeled herself, squaring her shoulders. 'I have work,' Antonio explained, knowing how lame it sounded. How lame it was. 'At the office.'

Maisie folded her arms, pursed her lips. She wasn't fooled. 'Blowing hot and cold still,' she said coolly, but her hurt and anger were betrayed by a tremble in her voice. 'You know, Antonio, I'd rather you just stayed away rather than lurch about, unsure whether you want to be in our lives or not. Make up your mind.'

Stung, Antonio drew back. He knew she was right, but it still hurt. 'Fine,' he said. 'I'll see you next week.'

And with that he strode out into the night.

CHAPTER ELEVEN

THE NEXT FEW weeks fell into a routine that felt, at different times, both pleasant and confusing. Maisie found she enjoyed making the villa a home, and every morning she'd take Ella out to browse the little shops and sit in the village square, sometimes ordering a coffee and drinking it in the sunshine.

She'd also found a mother-and-baby group that met locally, and, although the language barrier remained an issue, she was surprised at how well she could communicate with a combination of miming and broken English and Italian.

Ella seemed to have settled well, sleeping better at night and being less fretful during the day. Max had video-chatted with her several times and, although he remained concerned, Maisie couldn't mistake the relief in his eyes and voice at knowing that she was okay and he was free. She didn't blame him. He was young, upwardly mobile, and wanted to experience the best of life. She was happy for him, and she was enjoying life in Italy more than she had expected...except for one thing.

Antonio was the wild card in her life, the turbulent wave in an otherwise placid sea. After that first infuriating night when he'd left before eating dinner, he had returned a week later with a schedule of visits, which had seemed sensible but also rather cold and businesslike. He'd proposed visiting Ella every other day, in the evening, and also on Saturdays.

'But if you require further help, a nanny or babysitter, you must let me know.'

'Maybe I will at some point,' Maisie had answered. She'd stared down at the schedule of visits and couldn't keep from feeling disappointed and even hurt. She wanted them to be friends, but Antonio seemed determined to merely tolerate her for Ella's sake. It hurt more than she knew it should.

Antonio had also engaged an Italian tutor for her, a smiling grandmother who bounced Ella on her lap while Maisie ran through conversational phrases. Maisie was starting to make progress with her Italian, but her daughter's father felt as much a frustrating enigma as ever.

During his visits with Ella he could be charming and funny, interested and concerned. If she ever had an issue with anything, whether it was a leaky tap or needing a car, Antonio solved it with alacrity. When he'd had an SUV delivered to the drive, she'd been speechless. He'd merely shrugged.

Despite the acts of generosity and concern, he remained intentionally and irritatingly remote, a shutter coming down over his eyes whenever Maisie asked anything personal. His life was still very much his own; he visited her, and not the other way around.

All in all, she reflected as she sat by the pool one afternoon two weeks after she'd arrived, despite the luxury and the sunshine and the few friends she'd made, she felt restless and discontented, as if she wanted something more. She just didn't know what.

The sun was starting to sink beneath the fringe of plane trees, so Maisie scooped up Ella and headed inside. Antonio had stopped by yesterday for dinner, giving Ella her bath and singing to her before bedtime, so Maisie didn't expect him today, a fact which made her heart sink a little.

The truth was, she felt lonely. Six months, or now five and a half, felt like a very long time. If Antonio made more of an effort, let her in a little…but he didn't. Maisie knew she shouldn't care, because he wasn't the sort of man to pin her dreams on. A ruthless playboy, no matter how devoted a father he seemed, was not a good bet.

She'd just put Ella down to sleep, the house full of shadows and pools of lamplight, when a knock sounded on the door. Surprised, Maisie went to answer it—then stared in shock at Antonio standing there.

'I didn't think you were coming today,' she said. 'And in any case, Ella is asleep.'

'I didn't come for Ella.'

A shiver of apprehension and excitement rippled through her. Maisie stepped back from the door to let him inside. Now that she was looking at him properly, she saw how restless and even angry he seemed, his fists loosely clenched, the buttons of his shirt undone. Stubble grazed his jaw and his hair was rumpled. Despite the tension emanating from him, he looked utterly appealing. She took another step back, reminding herself how easily she'd fallen for him once before.

'What's going on, Antonio?'

'Do you have anything to drink?'

'Sorry, I don't.' She folded her arms. 'Why did you come here?'

He gave her a crooked smile as he strode into the living room and flung himself down on the sofa. 'Because I couldn't face being alone.'

Curiosity warred with compassion as Maisie perched on the sofa opposite him. 'Why not?'

He tilted his head up to stare at the ceiling. 'Do you know what day it is, Maisie?'

It took her a moment to realise, and then she did with a thud, a deep, sinking sensation inside her. 'It's the anniversary of your brother's death,' she said softly.

'And Ella's conception.' He lowered his head to laser her with that piercing blue gaze. 'Do you remember?'

Her mouth was dry, her heart thumping. 'Of course I do, Antonio. But I thought you didn't want to.'

'Just because of that one time I pretended not to know you?' His mouth quirked wryly.

'Not just that,' Maisie allowed. 'Other things.' She took a deep breath, her hands twisted together. 'Sometimes it seems as if you enjoy being with me, and sometimes…not. Sometimes,' she continued, her voice growing stronger, 'it seems as if you don't even like me.'

Antonio let out a hollow laugh. 'I like you, Maisie. I like you too damn much.'

It shouldn't thrill her, but it did. 'Then why…?'

'Do you think I'm a total bastard?'

The question made her blink. 'No…'

'Just somewhat of one?'

'No. I don't admire your business practices, but as a man…' She trailed off uncertainly. This conversation felt as intimate as the one they'd shared exactly a year ago, when she'd wandered into that office, and, unknowingly, into her future.

Antonio looked at her again, heat and something deeper and sadder visible in his gaze. 'As a man?'

'I don't know, Antonio. You haven't given me a chance to know you.'

'Because I don't think you'd like what you discovered.'

'Perhaps you should let me be the judge of that,' Maisie said softly. 'Because a lot of what I do see, I like and admire.' Antonio made a scoffing noise, and she continued, her voice growing steadier and stronger as she realised how much she believed what she was saying. 'You're loving and gentle and tender with Ella. And you're considerate and thoughtful with me, thinking of things I need before I even know I need them, and working to provide them.'

He shrugged his shoulders. 'Money.'

'Not just money. Time and effort and thought, as well. And you can be charming and funny—'

'A veneer.'

'A nice one, then. Why do you think so little of yourself, Antonio? What's haunting you?' Because something surely was, and Maisie longed to know what it was. To help and even free this man she'd come to care about, even if she hadn't meant or wanted to. Even if he'd been keeping his distance and she had too, both of them protecting their hearts. Or was she merely being fanciful, hopeful…? 'Is it your brother's death?' Maisie asked quietly.

Antonio was silent for a long time, his expression shuttering once more. Maisie didn't think he was going to answer, and her heart twisted. She wanted to know. She needed to know. Antonio was her baby's father and, more importantly, he was the only man in her life. She wanted to get closer to him, to help him if she could. *To love him?*

The question startled her. She didn't love Antonio. Of course she didn't. She didn't know him well enough for that depth of feeling. And yet, she acknowledged, part of her wanted to love him. Wanted to open her heart, because she'd always wanted to open her heart. To find a person to love…and to love her back. But surely that couldn't be Antonio. Nothing that had happened between them so far should make her think, hope, and yet…

'Maisie,' he finally said as her thoughts reeled, 'will you do me a favour?'

'A favour? What is it?'

He looked at her, his expression full of grief and appeal. 'Will you play for me?'

Maisie's mouth dropped open as she stared at him. Antonio knew he shouldn't have come here. It had been a reckless act, driven by desperation and a deep, endless grief he kept at bay, or tried to, for three hundred and sixty-four days of the year. On this night he let it out—and he didn't want to be alone. He wanted to be with Maisie.

'Play?' Maisie whispered. 'You mean…?'

'Your violin. I've never heard you play, and I'd like to.'

'I haven't played in months,' she admitted. 'Not since Ella…'

'Will you play for me?' He wanted to hear her. He wanted to be carried away by music, on the wings of another person's passion. Maisie's passion. And most of all, for a little while, he wanted to forget. 'Please?'

'All right,' she whispered, and she rose to retrieve her violin. Antonio closed his eyes, fighting against the tide of memory pulling him under, beckoning him to drown. One night a year he gave in to the regret and guilt, and yet it was so torturous.

The first strains swept over him in a symphony of sound and emotion. He recognised the aching, melancholy notes of *Adagio for Strings*, by the American composer Samuel Barber, and he let the music flood him, overwhelm and inhabit him.

It carried him away to that place of yearning and sadness he tried not to access, that split him right open and left him exposed and aching.

He didn't realise the music had stopped until he felt Maisie's hand on his damp cheek.

'Antonio…' His name on her lips was a plea, a promise. He kept his eyes closed, savouring her touch. Craving it, even though he knew he shouldn't. He'd tried to keep himself distant and safe and here he was, undoing all that work. Wanting to undo it. 'You seem so anguished,' she whispered, her palm caressing his cheek. 'So *trapped...*'

'I am trapped.' The words emerged from him in something close to a gasp. 'I'll never be free.'

'Why?' He didn't answer. Couldn't. 'Why do you blame yourself for your brother's death?' she asked, her voice both soft and urgent. 'That's the crux of it, isn't it?'

'It was a car accident.' He could hardly believe he was about to tell her the truth. 'You know about car accidents, don't you?'

A pause, a breath. 'Yes...'

'Reckless driver. A single moment. That's how it was for your parents, wasn't it?'

'Is that what happened with your brother, Antonio? Were you driving?'

'No, Paolo was. But I was driving the other car.' He kept his eyes clenched shut, not wanting to see the dawning horror and judgement he knew would be on her face. 'We were racing.'

'Racing...'

'Yes, racing. Extreme sports were our thing, our escape.' He was trying to justify his actions, and he knew he couldn't. 'My thing,' he amended. 'My escape. And I brought Paolo along. My parents fought a lot, and my father was depressed after losing his job. It was a way to leave all that behind, if only for a short time.'

'That seems understandable,' Maisie murmured, but she sounded cautious, and who could blame her? Perhaps she could guess what he was going to say next.

'Understandable or unimaginable?' Antonio let out a hoarse laugh, more a cry of pain. 'Paolo was five years younger than me. He looked up to me, for support and guidance, everything. And I led him to his death.'

'It was an accident, Antonio—'

'One that could have been so easily avoided. I urged him on, Maisie.' He opened his eyes, needing to punish himself by looking at her as he told her the truth. 'He didn't even want to race that day. I called him a coward. I egged him on.'

'You couldn't have realised—'

'No, but I should have. I should have known. I should have been careful instead of reckless. Should have thought of him rather than seeking my own stupid adrenaline rush.'

'So what happened?' Maisie asked quietly.

'It started to rain. He wanted to stop. I insisted we keep going—racing down an empty street in the middle of the night.' He shook his head, regret lancing through him yet again. 'It was crazy. So crazy. It was as if I couldn't think. Couldn't see sense. And because I was his big brother, he did what I said. He put his foot on the accelerator and jumped ahead of me.' He closed his eyes again, the images flashing against his lids, impossible to erase. 'The car spun out of control. I watched it happen. Saw it crash into a barrier, and then burst into flames.' He stopped, unable to go on even though he knew he had to. He'd never spoken to anyone about what he'd seen. Doing it now felt like an exorcism. 'Stood and did nothing as my brother burned to death.'

'Oh, Antonio.' Her voice was full of sorrow instead of judgement and for some inexplicable reason that made Antonio angry.

He shook off her palm and glared at her. 'Don't you understand?' he demanded. 'I as good as killed him.'

Maisie regarded him steadily, unfazed by his sneering

fury. 'I know you feel as if you did,' she said quietly, her gaze still on him, 'but you didn't.'

'You can't say that.'

'Why not?'

He shifted restlessly where he sat, her questions both infuriating and unsettling him. 'Because you weren't there. You didn't see. You don't know—'

'And you do? Why do you hate yourself so much, Antonio? Why can't you forgive yourself? You didn't know your brother was going to die. You never wanted to hurt him.'

'But I *did.*'

'What happened after your brother died?'

'What do you mean?'

'To your family.'

Her perception took his breath away. 'I ruined my family,' he said flatly. '*Ruined* it.'

'Based on what you said about your parents fighting and your father's depression, it seems it already had its problems.'

'I made it a thousand times worse.'

'Your brother's death made it a thousand times worse,' Maisie corrected. 'But it's been eleven years, Antonio. The grief never goes away, I know that, but you heal.' She reached for him again, her fingertips brushing his cheek. 'Why haven't you healed?'

The question blindsided him. No one had ever asked him before. No one had ever known to ask. He realised in that moment just how broken he was inside, and how Maisie saw it. She'd seen it since the night she'd first met him, and he'd hated that, but in this moment it almost felt freeing. She saw him, and she was still here.

'I don't know why I haven't,' he admitted in a jagged voice, his eyes closed. 'I just know it's true.'

'Healing only comes with forgiveness. You have to forgive yourself, Antonio. Even if there are people in your life who won't.'

'My parents hate me. They won't speak to me.' He tried to speak matter-of-factly and failed. 'They haven't spoken to me since Paolo's funeral.'

'That's not your fault.'

'Isn't it?'

'No.'

He opened his eyes, touched by the sincerity in her tone, and comforted by the sureness. 'How can you be such a good person, Maisie Dobson?' he asked quietly as he stared into her face, which was full of compassion and sorrow. 'You've endured so much hardship. How can you still be kind? How can you still believe that good things happen?'

'Because the alternative is too terrible,' she answered quietly. 'There would be no reason for living, no hope if I didn't believe that there was a purpose to the pain, hope amidst the suffering.'

'You're too good for me.' As soon as he said the words he knew how true they were. She was far too good for him. He'd corrupt her, ruin her, just as he had ruined his family. That was why he had stayed away.

Except he wasn't staying away now. No, he was leaning forward, taking her hands in his, needing to ground himself in the wonderful reality of her touch, her acceptance.

Maisie's eyes widened but she didn't move away, didn't drop his hands. She waited.

Everything felt suspended in that moment, taut with expectancy and even hope, something he hadn't felt in far too long.

'Maisie,' Antonio said, and it was both question and answer. Her lips parted but no sound came out, and then Antonio leaned forward and kissed her.

CHAPTER TWELVE

THE BRUSH OF Antonio's lips across hers felt like coming home. Maisie knew she wasn't the first person to think such a thing, but it was true. So true, in this moment when all her doubts and uncertainties were swept away by the honesty of Antonio's pain and the promise of his kiss.

He brought his hands up to cradle her face, the touch so tender it made Maisie ache, as they kissed and kissed, a communication of their souls. This felt so much deeper and more intimate than when they'd come together before, so much more profound, and yet it was only a kiss. Except it wasn't just a kiss; it was life-giving and receiving, on and on.

Eventually Antonio tore his mouth from hers, his hand still framing her face as he looked into her eyes. 'Maisie…'

'I want this, Antonio.' She pressed her hand to his cheek, feeling utterly sure. 'I want this so much.'

He didn't need to be told twice. He rose from the sofa and, taking her by the hand, led her upstairs. The house was dark and quiet all around them, everything hushed and expectant. In her bedroom, Antonio dropped her hand and Maisie turned to him, waiting, ready and sure.

Antonio drew her to him and kissed her softly, tenderly. Maisie closed her eyes. Everything about this felt different from before, when things between them had been urgent, desperate, and more than a little sad.

Now, amidst the burgeoning passion and need, Maisie felt an unfurling of hope, of happiness, and she thought Antonio felt it too. Surely he couldn't kiss her this way, so reverently, if he didn't.

He was kissing her with such tenderness and sweet passion that Maisie's heart flipped over and melted, everything in her straining and yearning as she pressed her body against his and offered him everything.

Clothes slipped off seemingly by themselves; a whisper of cloth, the snick of a button or zip. Antonio's body was beautiful, burnished by moonlight, the lambent light catching his perfectly sculpted muscles.

He pulled back the duvet and then reached for her hand; they lay down in a splayed tangle of limbs, hands and mouths seeking each other as the rest of the world dropped away.

Maisie arched and writhed under Antonio's knowing yet tender touch, marvelling at how well he knew her, how he discovered her secret places and brought her to glittering precipices of pleasure over and over again until she finally fell among the shards, crying out as her body convulsed under his.

He rolled on top of her, reaching for a condom from the pocket of his trousers as Maisie gave a throaty laugh.

'You came prepared.'

'It never hurts.'

Seconds later he sank inside her, and Maisie closed her eyes as he filled her right up, and they began to move in exquisite, joined rhythm, climbing towards those dazzling heights yet again.

Afterwards, Antonio wrapped his arms around her as he rolled onto his back, taking her with him. She felt cocooned by his embrace, safe and protected in a way she couldn't remember feeling for such a long time. She wasn't in charge. She didn't need to cling to her control. She could just be held.

Neither of them spoke, but then Maisie didn't think they needed to say anything. At some point she fell into a sated doze, only to startle awake when she heard Ella's plaintive cry.

'I'll get her,' Antonio murmured in her ear, and carefully he disentangled himself from her. Still sleepy, Maisie curled up in the warm space left in the bed as Antonio pulled on his boxers and went in search of their daughter.

She dozed again, only to wake at the low, thrumming sound of Antonio singing. Holding her breath, Maisie listened for a few moments before she grabbed her dressing gown and belted it around her waist, then tiptoed down the corridor to Ella's room.

Antonio held his daughter in one powerful arm, rocking her gently as he sang a lullaby in Italian, his baritone caressing the musical syllables. Ella blinked up at him, transfixed, and Maisie's heart swelled with both love and gratitude. She wouldn't trade this moment for the world. She just wished she could hold on to it.

Antonio swayed slightly as he sang, and Maisie watched as Ella's eyelids began to droop. Another few moments and then her daughter was asleep, and Antonio laid her gently in the cot.

He caught Maisie's eye as he straightened, and smiled. Maisie smiled back, feeling yet another welling-up of love and thankfulness, almost painful in its intensity. It was scary to feel this much. To want this much.

Because in that moment she wanted Antonio. Not just as a lover or a friend, but as a partner. A soulmate. The realisation jolted her, a bolt of terror lancing right through her, and the smile dropped from her face.

Antonio frowned, catching the change in mood, and in silence they walked back to her bedroom.

'Thank you,' Maisie began haltingly. 'For...for rocking her to sleep.'

Antonio shrugged. 'It's the least I can do. You have the far greater burden of care.'

'It's no burden.' Too late Maisie realised she sounded prickly, but the truth was, she didn't know how to feel, when the realisation of how much she wanted Antonio, how much she hoped for, left her feeling flayed and raw. They'd shared an intense evening, but had it been real? Could she trust this man? Did she want to? She'd always had so much love to give, but she knew how much it hurt when you lost that love. Her parents' death, Antonio's previous rejection... She felt wary now, and that made her defensive.

'I didn't mean that.' Antonio gazed at her appraisingly and Maisie tightened the sash of her dressing gown, battling too many different emotions.

'I should go.' The words were abrupt, firm. Maisie blinked in surprise. Somehow she hadn't expected that, but why not? Despite the tenderness Antonio had just shown her, had he really changed? He was ruthless. A playboy. He made no bones about it. She'd had an epiphany tonight, but it didn't mean he had.

'Okay,' she said at last, and something flickered across Antonio's face before he turned away. Maisie watched him dress, uncertain as to what to say. Were they going to discuss what had happened, or just pretend it hadn't? Which did she want?

Antonio finished dressing in silence and then headed downstairs. Maisie followed him, watching as he shrugged on his coat and jangled his keys.

'When will you be back? To visit Ella, I mean,' she clarified quickly, a flush rising to her face.

Antonio's mouth twisted. 'I know what you meant. I'll come on Saturday, as I usually do.'

'Shall we spend the day together?' Maisie tried not to sound too hopeful. They'd spent the last few Saturdays together, exploring the countryside, but maybe things had changed now. Perhaps Antonio wanted them to change.

Antonio hesitated, his gaze moving over her face. 'Perhaps it would be better if I took Ella out on her own.'

Maisie's stomach plunged with disappointment. 'But I'll have to feed her.'

'Couldn't you make up a bottle?'

'She hasn't had a bottle yet.'

'She's over three months old. It seems sensible to start.'

Maisie opened her mouth to argue, What did Antonio know about babies and bottles? but then she closed it again. He was right; if he was going to take their daughter out on his own, Ella would need to get used to bottles. But Maisie didn't like any of it, couldn't help but feel hurt.

'Fine,' she said. Antonio nodded, and then he opened the door and was gone. Maisie sagged against the wall, her body and heart both aching. How had that gone so disastrously wrong? And what had she been expecting or at least hoping to happen, really?

She stayed there for a few minutes, her head spinning, the house quiet and dark all around her. Then slowly she went upstairs; the bed was still rumpled and the sheets smelled of him. Maisie dragged in a quick, hitched breath and willed herself not to cry.

It was better this way. She knew what it was like to love and lose. The months and even years after her parents' sudden death had left her with gaping wounds inside, wounds that had only just begun to heal. Could she even contemplate caring for someone else, and having those wounds ripped open?

Antonio was right to keep their relationship briskly businesslike. Tonight had been an aberration. A wonderful and devastating one.

Maisie climbed into bed and pulled the duvet right up over her head. For a few hours she wanted to block out the world. If only she could do the same with her memories. As it was, she lay in bed, her eyes scrunched shut, everything in her aching, as sleep refused to come.

'Antonio!'

Maisie's smile of surprised delight sucker-punched Antonio right in the gut. He smiled back, trying to maintain his slightly remote composure. Yes, he was here a day early, but it didn't have to mean anything.

'I wasn't expecting you until tomorrow,' Maisie said as Antonio dropped his suit jacket and stretched out next to her and Ella on the blanket spread on the sun-dappled grass. The water of the pool sparkled in the sunlight and the smell of orange blossom wafted on the gentle breeze. It was a beautiful day, peaceful and pleasant, and a far cry from the grimy hustle and bustle of Milan's business district.

'I know you weren't, but I ended up with some free time and I wanted to see Ella.' Maisie's face fell but she quickly reassembled her cheerful expression, giving him a smile.

'I'm glad, and she is too, obviously.'

Antonio smiled down at his daughter and tickled her bare feet, earning a delighted grin and a little baby gurgle of laughter, the sound of simple joy wrapping around his heart and squeezing. Hard.

The truth was, he couldn't have kept away if he'd tried,

which he hadn't. He'd wanted to be here, under the fig tree, in the sunlight, with Ella and Maisie. His family. The word wrapped around his heart with another breathless squeeze. How could he be thinking such a thing, never mind actually hoping for it? Was he crazy? Hadn't he learned?

'The other reason I'm here,' he said, still gazing down at Ella, 'is that a client of mine had tickets to see an opera at La Scala tonight and I thought you might like to go.'

'To the opera?' He glanced up to see Maisie goggling at him.

'Yes.'

'With…with you?'

'Yes, with me.' Antonio managed a wry smile. The truth was, a client hadn't given him the tickets. He'd bought them himself, because he thought Maisie would enjoy attending, and he'd wanted to go with her. Be with her. That impulse, that need, had trumped every other precaution or concern or doubt. For now.

'I'd love to go, but…' Maisie bit her lip. 'What about Ella?'

'I can arrange a babysitter for her. We can leave after she's fallen asleep.' He smiled, cocking his head. 'You have to do it some time, you know.'

'I know. And I did try with a bottle this morning and it was fine…'

'There you are, then.'

Her face lit up, and then immediately fell. 'I have nothing to wear.'

'That,' Antonio assured her, 'is easily remedied. And in any case, you don't need to dress in a particularly fancy way. Doing so will only make you look like a tourist.'

Maisie laughed as she brushed a curly strand of hair from her eyes. 'Heavens, we wouldn't want that!'

'No, indeed.'

Just a few hours later they were settled in a limo, driving to see *La Traviata* at La Scala in Milan. The babysitter, the grandmotherly woman who had been teaching Maisie Italian, was entirely at ease with Ella—allowing Maisie to relax. Antonio saw the sparkle in her eyes as she strained to catch a glimpse of the iconic building.

She wore a dress of soft black jersey that clung to her womanly curves and made Antonio ache to touch her. All afternoon and evening he'd battled with himself, caught between wanting to be careful and simply wanting Maisie. To be with her, to talk to her, to touch her. It was more than a matter of craving; it was his soul's need. And he wasn't going to examine it farther than that. Not tonight, at least.

'Wow,' Maisie breathed as they took their seats in a private box in the theatre, with its plush red velvet and ornate gold decoration. 'Antonio, this is amazing.'

'I'm glad you think so.' He loved watching her take it all in, the pleasure that lit her from within. He was glad he'd bought the tickets, glad he'd come here. Glad, so glad, he was with her.

The lights dimmed and the first notes of the opera swelled. Maisie gave him an excited little smile. Antonio returned the grin, then settled back to watch the opera… and Maisie.

As the opera continued, Antonio found he couldn't take his eyes off her. She was enchanting and so very lovely, enraptured by every note and movement, talking non-stop during the intermission as they sipped champagne in the elegant foyer.

'Sorry, sorry,' she said with a laugh when she paused to take a breath. 'I'm rabbiting on…'

'No,' Antonio assured her. 'I love listening to you.'

A small, surprised smile stole across her face and Antonio smiled back, determined not to give in to his fears. Wanting to be different.

Several hours later they walked out into the starry night, to his limo waiting at the kerb.

'That was so incredible,' Maisie said in a dreamy voice. 'And the story was so sad.'

'Aren't all operas sad?'

'I suppose so, although I've never actually been to the opera before.'

'Me neither.'

'Really?' She shot him a curious look as she slid into the limo. 'I assumed you've done just about everything.'

'No, this is new.' Too late he realised the double meaning of his words. This was new. Them. Antonio saw realisation flare in Maisie's eyes, and he struggled with the urge to take it all back. Close it down.

Somehow he didn't. The silence stretched on as he got in the car and the driver pulled out into the traffic. Antonio glanced at Maisie; her cheek looked soft and round, the moonlight catching its silky curve, as she gazed out of the window.

'I have a charity gala to attend this weekend,' he said abruptly, and Maisie turned to him, eyebrows raised.

'A charity gala?'

'Yes, on Saturday. Why don't you come with me?'

Pleasure and uncertainty warred in her lovely, expressive features. 'You want me to…?'

'Yes.'

'All right.' She smiled shyly, the sparkle returning to her eyes. 'Is it formal, though? Because then I really don't have anything to wear.'

'Sounds like you need a shopping trip in Milan, then,' Antonio answered lightly. 'How about tomorrow?'

'But Ella…'

'I'll come as well. I can hold her while you try on gowns.'

'All right.' A smile bloomed on Maisie's face and in his heart. He found he was already looking forward to tomorrow. To a whole lot of tomorrows.

CHAPTER THIRTEEN

MAISIE GAZED AT her reflection in the mirror, amazed at her appearance. She felt utterly transformed, not just by the evening gown she'd picked out yesterday at a boutique that had been more luxurious than any shop she'd ever imagined, but also by her new hair and make-up.

Antonio had arranged for a stylist to come to the house and Maisie had been both flattered and worried that he thought she needed the help of a professional to pass muster at an event like this one.

And maybe she did, because the truth was, Maisie felt out of her league. Going to La Scala had already been a step up, but this, a party full of socialites and businessmen, a place where she'd have to impress, felt like entering another stratosphere. It was hard to breathe.

The truth was, Antonio was out of her league, something that felt all too apparent now. It wasn't so obvious when she was eating her body weight in spaghetti while they chatted at the dinner table, or when Antonio was tickling Ella's feet or giving her a bottle. Safely cocooned in the haven that her villa had become, she felt Antonio's equal, if not necessarily his partner. And as excited as she was to attend an elegant party on Antonio's arm, she was also terrified. The last time she'd been at a party she'd been pouring the champagne. What if she messed up? What if she was laughed at? What if she made Antonio regret bringing her not just to the party, but to Italy as well?

'Maisie?' His voice, low and melodious, rippled over her senses. Maisie straightened her shoulders, giving her reflection one last glance. She looked good, better than she ever had before. She could take confidence in that, at least, even if she was nervous and uncertain about everything else…including Antonio himself.

Yesterday, shopping with him had been so much fun, trying on and twirling around in various evening gowns, while he had held Ella and rated them from one to ten, nearly all of them coming in at ten or nine and a half. Maisie hadn't missed the heat flaring in his eyes when he'd looked at her, and a thrill had run through her every time.

He hadn't touched her since the night of the anniversary of his brother's death, even though Maisie had been hoping for a goodnight kiss after the opera. No, Antonio was keeping his distance that way, even if he was spending more time with her. He was still blowing hot and cold, and Maisie didn't know what to do about it. How patient to be. How much to hope for. And where her self-respect fitted into all this, because she knew, in her heart, she was waiting for Antonio to make up his mind. And that wasn't that great a feeling.

'Maisie,' Antonio said again, and now there was a note of affectionate exasperation in his voice that made Maisie smile. She unlocked the door to the bedroom, and did a little, nervous twirl.

'You look magnificent,' Antonio said, and Maisie thrilled to the husky note in his voice.

'Has the babysitter arrived?' she asked, mainly because she didn't know how to respond to him when he was looking at her with such blatant male appreciation. And she knew she was looking at him with similar appreciation, for he looked devastatingly attractive in his midnight-black tuxedo, the crisp white shirt contrasting with his bronzed skin and dark hair, his eyes looking bluer and more piercing than ever.

'Yes, the babysitter's here,' he said. 'She's waiting in the living area.' He took her hand and drew her to him. 'There's no need to worry. Ella was fine the other night, and she'll be fine tonight, as well. We can enjoy ourselves.'

Which made it sound like a date. Antonio was certainly looking at her as if it was a date. After the happiness of the last few days, Maisie was too afraid to ask if it was. Maybe it was wrong or at least pathetic to take what few crumbs Antonio tossed her way, but she felt like Cinderella tonight and she wanted Antonio to be her prince…for a night. That was all she'd let herself dream of.

'I have something for you,' Antonio said, and Maisie blinked in surprise as he withdrew a slim box of black velvet from the inside pocket of his jacket. He presented it to her, snapping the box open with a flourish, and Maisie sucked in a breath of shocked delight at the emerald and diamond choker nestled in satin.

'Antonio, it's too much…'

'It's perfect for your dress,' he replied, dismissing her half-hearted protest. She'd never seen such a beautiful piece of jewellery, never mind worn one. 'Let me,' Antonio murmured, and obediently Maisie turned around so he could clasp the choker around her neck.

His fingers brushed the tender skin of her nape and shivers rippled outward as she drew a sharp breath in, trying to curb the heady desire that rushed through her at the simple touch. The last few days had been a torture of unsated desire, remembering their night together and longing for another one.

If she were braver, she would have taken matters into

her own hands, turned around to face him—and to kiss him. But she wasn't that brave. She still didn't know how he felt, not truly. Although they'd spent more time together, Antonio was still changeable, still occasionally remote. And, Maisie had realised, she'd done the heavy lifting in relationships so much in her life. For once she wanted Antonio to show her how he felt. How important she was to him. But perhaps he never would, because she wasn't. She still didn't know.

The clasp done, Antonio rested his hands on her bare shoulders, his palms warm and sure against her skin as his breath fanned the back of her neck. Maisie closed her eyes, nearly swaying with need for him. Hope and desire tangled together as memories raced through her mind of their night together, the tenderness Antonio had shown, the honesty he'd given her with both his body and his words. Would he—could he—give it again?

Neither of them spoke, the only sound their mingled breath. Then Antonio pressed a kiss to the back of her neck, and Maisie trembled. It was so little, and yet so much.

'We should go,' he murmured, and she tried to make her legs less jelly-like as she turned around to face him. His eyes were opaque, his expression inscrutable, but he gave her the tiniest quirk of a smile as he took her hand and led her from the room.

Soon they were heading outside into the dark, balmy night, the warm air silky against Maisie's skin.

She slid into the dim, luxurious interior of the waiting limo, and Antonio sat next to her, the long, hard length of his thigh pressing against her in a way that agitated her senses all over again.

'How come you never drive?' she asked as the limo pulled into Milan's night traffic. 'You always have a limo or at least a driver.'

Antonio drummed his fingers on the armrest, his gaze on the blur of buildings streaming by outside, as he answered, 'I haven't driven in over ten years.'

It didn't take more than a second for Maisie to realise what he meant. 'You mean since your brother's death,' she stated softly, and Antonio gave a terse nod.

Maisie's heart twisted inside her. 'You've been tormented by his death for so long, Antonio,' she said quietly. 'When are you going to let it go?'

'I can't.' His face was still averted. 'I've tried, and you've helped, by listening.' His voice was tight and suffocated, and Maisie knew how hard this was for him. She wanted to comfort him and assure him that he didn't need to feel guilty, but she sensed that Antonio was reaching his limit for this kind of conversation. So she settled for simply putting her hand on his arm, and after a second's pause Antonio rested his hand on top of hers. Neither of them spoke, and they stayed that way until the limo pulled up in front of the opulent hotel where the charity gala was being held.

As Maisie left the limo and walked up the wide marble steps to the hotel her heart felt as if it would burst out of her chest. Pride and joy pulsed through her and she couldn't keep from shooting Antonio a glance of pure happiness and excitement. He smiled back, and her heart sang.

As they stepped through the hotel's doors he leaned forward and murmured, 'I already know you will be the most beautiful woman here tonight.'

Maisie's chin lifted another notch and she straightened her shoulders as she sailed through the doors on Antonio's arm.

The evening had only just begun and it was already spinning out of control. Already, at least a dozen times in the last few days, Antonio had broken his resolution to be remote. It had started when he'd stayed for dinner two nights ago, and then continued when he'd invited Maisie to La Scala, and then shopping, and now this ball. He kept upping the ante when he should have folded. The stakes were simply too high. And yet here he was. Here *they* were.

Instead of moving away from Maisie, he was moving towards her, and no more so than now, when he walked into a roomful of colleagues and acquaintances with her on his arm.

And, although part of him was muttering that he was being a dangerous fool, Antonio couldn't regret a thing. Maisie looked radiant, her lovely, heart-shaped face full of joy, her eyes shining like jade stars. And he was proud to be on her arm. Proud and delighted.

Within moments they were swept up in the crowd, and Antonio began introducing her to various people he knew. He didn't mention Ella or the nature of his relationship to Maisie, although he could sense people's surprise. He normally came to events such as this one alone, not wanting to complicate things or raise the expectations of his ever-so-brief liaisons. The simple fact of Maisie's presence was cause enough for people to take note.

And, although he knew she'd been nervous to attend such a glittering event, Maisie held her own marvellously. Her natural warmth and generous nature attracted people to her, even the skinny socialites who were normally quick to unsheathe their claws. Antonio's pride and delight both grew.

Halfway through the evening Antonio was called into a private conversation with a business associate, and he watched, distracted, as Maisie was swept up by the crowd. He wasn't worried, not exactly, but he didn't like her being on her own.

'You certainly seem smitten,' Raoul, his business associate, remarked drily. 'I've never seen you with a woman before, Antonio. You usually avoid them unless there's a bed near by.'

Antonio winced, even though he knew it was true. 'Maisie isn't like that.'

'And neither are you, it seems. Tell me, is it serious?'

Antonio met Raoul's laughing gaze, suddenly stricken. Of course it wasn't *serious*. They weren't even dating, no matter what had happened three nights ago. The memory of it was still imprinted on his mind, his soul. And yet... despite that, despite everything, he'd somehow managed to deceive himself that he wasn't changing their status. He certainly wasn't starting to care about Maisie. He just liked being with her.

'Now you're looking like a rabbit trapped in a snare,' Raoul said with a laugh. 'And here I was, thinking I was pointing out the obvious.'

'It's...' Antonio's mind spun. He didn't want to denigrate Maisie in any way by saying he didn't care for her, and yet... *how could he*? How could he risk that much, when he knew how much love hurt, how much you lost when it was gone? When he knew, as sure as anything he'd ever known, that he would end up hurting Maisie because he'd hurt everyone he'd ever cared about? 'It's a complicated situation,' he finally said, making his tone repressive. 'But I esteem Maisie highly. Very highly indeed.'

Later, when he'd finished his conversation, he went in search of her, and found her standing in the corner, clutching a glass of champagne and looking thoughtful.

'Are you having a good time?' he asked as he stood beside her, unable to keep from slipping an arm around her slender waist.

'Yes, I have been. Very much so.' She sounded hesitant, and Antonio didn't like that.

'Dance with me,' he said, mostly because he wanted to feel her body next to his. She came willingly, and as they stepped onto the dance floor Antonio put his arms around her and drew her snugly into his embrace.

They swayed silently for a few minutes to the strings of the orchestra, neither of them speaking. Antonio glanced down at Maisie and saw her forehead was furrowed in thought. Gently he placed a finger under her chin and tilted her face up so she was looking at him.

'What is it, Maisie?' he asked.

'What do you mean?'

'You seem troubled.'

'Not troubled.'

'Then…?'

She hesitated, her lips pressed together, her wide green gaze trained on him. 'While you were talking to that businessman…'

Something remarkably like fear clutched at Antonio's chest. 'Yes?'

'People were talking. About you.'

He felt cold, although he kept his voice steady and light as he answered. 'And?'

'They were saying things. Things you've never explained…'

What on earth was he meant to explain? What had they said? Antonio didn't think he wanted to know. 'What kind of things?'

'Good things,' Maisie burst out, shocking him. 'Antonio, they were telling me how this business of yours—acting as a consultant when businesses are being taken over—is actually *charitable*. That you come in and try to minimise the impact of the takeover on all the employees, even the cleaners. That people have said they owe their lives to you.' Antonio stared at her dumbly, shocked that it was actually good things she'd heard. 'Why didn't you tell me?' she asked in a quieter voice. 'Here I was, getting false information from ridiculous tabloids and thinking you were a heartless monster who only cared about making a profit.'

'Profits are important—'

'One man,' Maisie cut across him, fierce now, 'explained that you don't actually make any money from this service. When companies hire you to smooth over the transition period, you add your consulting fee to the severance packages of the employees whose jobs are being cut. You don't get anything. You take time off from your own work to help other businesses, other people.' It was all true, so he simply nodded. 'Why didn't you tell me?' Maisie cried softly. 'Correct me? I had it so, so wrong, and I let it colour my perception of you.'

'And has your perception changed?'

'Of course it has.'

'How?'

'Because…because I know you're a good man. Not just with your own child, which I saw before, but in every way. Before now I had to reconcile the man I knew, the man who held me so tenderly, who cuddled Ella and cared about every little thing, with the ruthless businessman the media portray you to be. And now I don't have to do that any more.' Her eyes sparkled with tears as she smiled. 'I know who you are.'

Antonio felt as if she'd sucker-punched him with that clear, pure statement. She'd grabbed his heart and wasn't letting go, because she was right. She did know him, and she was still here. Still smiling at him. He'd told her his worst secrets and she'd discovered his best, and she was *here.*

'Let's leave this party,' he said, his voice a growl of intent.

'Leave…?'

'I want to be alone with you.'

Colour suffused Maisie's face and a small smile curved those lips he already felt the burning need to taste. 'All right,' she whispered. Antonio didn't wait for more. Taking her by the hand, he led her off the dance floor, out of the hotel and into the night.

CHAPTER FOURTEEN

'GOOD MORNING.'

Maisie blinked sleepily in the early sunlight, her body aching rather deliciously from the long bout of lovemaking she and Antonio had shared last night. There had been no words between them as they'd driven home, because there hadn't needed to be. Everything had felt expectant, exciting, and yet also supremely peaceful. For once Maisie had had no doubts, no worries, no fears.

Back at the villa Antonio had dismissed the babysitter and the very second the door had closed behind her Maisie was in his arms. Whether she or Antonio had moved first, she couldn't have said. It didn't matter. Their bodies and lips and even their souls had met in perfect, harmonious accord…and remained so for most of the night.

But, now that bright sunlight was streaming through the windows, Maisie was conscious of her incredible bed-head, especially given how unforgivably sexy Antonio looked wearing only a pair of drawstring pyjama bottoms, hair mussed, his eyes sparkling as he held two mugs of coffee… She felt happy, but she also fought a needle-like pinprick of doubt. What was going to happen now? Because she knew, with a leaden certainty, that Antonio was still calling the shots. Perhaps he always would be.

'Where's Ella?' she asked, her tone turning anxious as

she realised how late in the morning it had to be. Ella was usually awake by six.

'Napping.'

'But—'

'I woke up with her and gave her one of the bottles you'd made up that were in the fridge. She went back to sleep a little while ago. She's fine.'

'Oh.' Maisie sat back against the pillows, drawing the duvet up to cover her breasts and then pushing a wild hank of hair out of her eyes, surprised and shyly pleased by Antonio's actions.

'Is that okay?' Antonio asked as he handed her a cup of coffee and sat down next to her, the musky scent of him invading her senses as the mattress bowed beneath his weight.

'Yes, of course.' Maisie took a much-needed sip of coffee and murmured, 'Thank you.'

'It was my pleasure, as well as my duty. You wake up with Ella every morning.'

'I don't mind—'

'I know you don't.' He rested one hand on her arm, his fingers curving around her wrist. 'But I don't, either.'

Maisie took another sip of coffee, steeling herself for the conversation she knew they needed to have. She couldn't go on this way, seesawing between hope and fear, wondering if anything had really changed this time, or if Antonio was going to suddenly turn remote and chilly. Surely knowing was better than not, and yet…she was afraid to know. To have it end.

'Antonio, what happens now?' she asked quietly.

He arched an eyebrow. 'Now?'

'Now, today, tomorrow, for ever. Well, not for ever,' she clarified hastily, wishing she hadn't said something so stupid. She didn't want Antonio to think she was thinking in those terms.

'You mean between us.' He stated the words quietly, his gaze both appraising and inscrutable. She had no idea what he thought about it. About them.

'Yes, between us. Things keep changing—one day I feel very close to you, and the next...' She spoke haltingly, cringing inwardly at how vulnerable she was being and yet knowing she needed to say this. She needed answers. She needed knowledge. And yet it felt so very exposing, so incredibly raw, to admit as much. It felt weak too, because surely she should be calling the shots or at least trying to, rather than just giving Antonio all the power. The trouble was, she didn't know how to do that. How to be that strong.

'The next you don't.' Antonio spoke matter-of-factly, a flat note in his voice that made Maisie cringe even more.

'Well...yes.' She examined his face, searching his features for some hint as to how he felt about what she was saying, about *her*.

'I'm sorry,' Antonio said after a moment. 'I know I haven't been exactly fair.'

'I don't know if it's a question of fair. It's just... I need to know how you feel. What you want.' She swallowed painfully. 'Even if it's difficult...for both of us.'

Antonio didn't answer for a long moment. 'Sometimes I don't know how I feel,' he finally said in a low voice. 'Or what I want.'

'Okay,' Maisie said after a pause, fighting a wash of disappointment at his obvious ambivalence. What had she expected? For Antonio to pull her into his arms and declare his undying love? Yeah, right.

'I don't know what I feel,' Antonio continued, 'because I haven't let myself feel anything for so long. Years. Decades.'

'Since Paolo's death,' Maisie clarified softly.

'Yes.' He met her gaze steadily, but she could tell it cost him.

'So if you let yourself feel,' she asked, her throat aching and her heart thumping, 'what would you feel?'

The question hung in the air between them, suspended, the moment endless.

'I don't know,' Antonio said at last, and once again Maisie fought the flood of disappointment. Stupid to feel it, she knew. She could hardly expect Antonio to proclaim he loved her...could she? Just because she was starting to fall for him, a relentless tumble that was snowballing faster and faster as she learned more about him. Learned that he wasn't the ruthless businessman she'd assumed he was, not by a long shot. And maybe he wasn't the careless playboy, either, even though he'd certainly given that impression. But none of that meant he loved her. Not remotely.

'What I do know,' Antonio said, his voice growing stronger, 'is that I don't want us to have some businesslike relationship. For Ella's sake, as well as for our sakes. We have a chemistry, Maisie, and more than that. I don't want to walk away from what we have...what we could have.'

'So...' She licked her dry lips. 'Are you saying you want to...to have a relationship?'

For a moment Antonio looked trapped, with the classic deer-in-the-headlights widening of his eyes, so much so that Maisie almost laughed. Almost. Then he nodded slowly. 'Yes,' he said, the word seeming as if it had to be dragged from him. 'That's what I'm saying.'

Maisie nodded back, and they sipped coffee for a few minutes, both of them absorbing the tectonic shift in their relationship, letting it sink in. Then Ella started to cry, and Maisie felt relieved to slide out of bed and go to her, because the truth was she didn't know how to *be* with Antonio right then.

The next hour was spent settling Ella, and then showering and getting dressed, all the time avoiding Antonio, or trying to. When she finally came downstairs with Ella in her arms, fighting both apprehension and shyness, Antonio was waiting in the kitchen with a picnic basket and a blanket.

'I thought we could go to Lake Lugano,' he said with an easy smile. 'Have a picnic. It's only about an hour from here.'

Maisie blinked at him in surprise. 'Don't you have to work?'

'I can take a day off.'

A whole day with Antonio…as a family. Hope and happiness bloomed in Maisie's heart. 'All right,' she said, smiling back at him. 'That's great.'

Moments later the basket and blanket were in the back of the car Antonio had provided for her, and with Ella buckled in her car seat, kicking her legs happily, they were off, cruising along the narrow, hilly lanes that cut through the glacier-made valleys of Northern Italy. Maisie had taken the wheel, since she knew of Antonio's aversion to driving; it felt surprisingly natural to drive along, chatting all the way.

'Lake Lugano is on the border between Italy and Switzerland,' Antonio said as they crawled through the centre of a sleepy village. 'Over half of it is in Switzerland, actually, but we'll stay on the Italian side, I think, since it's closer.'

Soon enough the shimmering, deep blue waters of the lake were spread out before them, and Antonio directed her to a car park in a little commune. With Ella in the stroller they walked on a promenade that ran along the shores of the lake, the air balmy and warm, the day near-perfect. The uncertainties and apprehension Maisie had been feeling were swept away like cobwebs, and everything felt clean and new again.

Antonio seemed relaxed too, his hands in his pockets as they walked along, talking about everything and nothing, sometimes bending down to chuck Ella's chin or tickle her toes. Her daughter's happy, answering gurgle was a song in Maisie's heart. She didn't think anything could be more wonderful. If this was a sign of things to come, of the life she'd share with Antonio, then she'd have no worries at all. No fears lurking in the dark corners of her newly swept heart. Everything, absolutely everything, felt possible.

This was happiness. Antonio had to keep reminding himself, because it felt so unnatural. So tenuous. He kept glancing at Maisie and Ella, waiting for them to disappear like the mirages they seemed to be, or at least for a frown to mar the perfect smoothness of Maisie's forehead. Surely something would go wrong.

Or maybe it would simply go wrong in him, because as the day stretched on, golden and perfect, Antonio felt himself get more and more tense, increasingly restless. He tried to stop it, tried to revel in the simple pleasure of being with Maisie and Ella, but he couldn't. Perhaps he just wasn't made that way. Perhaps he'd been ruined along with his brother, his family, and there was no hope for him after all.

They ate lunch on a stretch of soft grass by the lake, bumblebees and butterflies lazily tumbling through the air, the only sound the distant buzz of a motorboat. Maisie fed Ella and then put her in the stroller for a nap, her chubby face covered by a sunshade.

She and Antonio stretched out on the blanket, legs tangled together, and lazed in the sun. Everything about it should have been wonderful but it wasn't. Despite his best intentions Antonio couldn't let himself relax. Couldn't make himself hope.

'Antonio.' Maisie's voice was gentle, but he still heard

the faint reproach. She laid her palm against his cheek as she gazed into his eyes. 'What is it? Why are you so jumpy?'

'I don't know.' He shifted onto his back so her hand fell away. 'This is new for me, Maisie. I haven't had a proper relationship in years, like I told you.' Actually, he'd never really had a proper romantic relationship. Had never even wanted to try.

'I know it's new. It's new for me too.' Her voice was soft and sad, making him feel worse—and even jumpier. 'It's okay,' she added. 'We don't have to rush things, Antonio. We can just take each day as it comes.'

He stared up at the sky, the bright blue starting to fade at the edges. In her stroller, Ella stirred. 'We should go,' he said. 'It's getting late, and I really should get to the office at some point today.'

'Okay.'

He didn't look at her as he stood up; Maisie began packing away the picnic things and Antonio folded the blanket. Neither of them spoke as they walked back to the car, and it wasn't the companionable silence of earlier. Things felt tense, unhappy, as if they were already unravelling. And Antonio knew it was all his fault.

'I'm sorry,' he said after they'd spent an hour of tense silence in the car, and they'd pulled into the drive of Maisie's villa. 'I wanted this day to be perfect.'

Maisie gave him a wry smile, her eyes shadowed. 'Nothing's perfect, but I enjoyed today, Antonio. Truly.'

How could she be so patient with him? Somehow it made him feel worse. He'd already called his driver to pick him up, and the limo pulled up to the kerb before he answered Maisie. 'I'll see you soon,' he said, keeping it vague on purpose. He quickly kissed Ella's forehead before striding towards the limo. As he slid into the leather interior, he couldn't keep from breathing a sigh of relief. At least now he didn't have to feel as if he was failing all the time.

Antonio spent the next few days working, communicating with Maisie only by text and trying not to feel guilty that once again he was taking a step back, out of necessity more than anything else. Yet that first burst of relief he'd felt had quickly evaporated, leaving him so restless and ill-tempered that even his staff noticed.

He wasn't happy with Maisie, and he wasn't happy without her. Relationships were impossible for him. All of it made Antonio furious with himself, and even more irritable, until people started to noticeably avoid him. Finally, three days after their trip to Lake Lugano, he broke down and headed towards Maisie's villa.

Dusk was falling as the car pulled into the drive. Antonio dismissed his driver and got out, straightening his jacket as well as his resolve. He glimpsed Maisie through the window, Ella in her arms, her fiery hair pulled back in a messy bun, her body slender and supple as she soothed their baby. As Antonio opened the front door he heard the soft, melodious notes of a lullaby; Maisie's voice was as lovely as her playing of the violin.

He paused there for a moment, savouring the beauty and peace of the scene—the dim, lamplit room, the enticing smells of basil and garlic emanating from the kitchen, Maisie's sweet voice as she sang to their daughter. It was all so warm and welcoming, so wonderful, and so unlike the cold life, impersonal and sterile, that Antonio had constructed for himself over the last ten years. He wondered why on earth he'd stayed away for the last few days.

'Maisie?' he called, and she came around the corner, her lovely face wreathed in smiles.

'Antonio.' There was nothing but joy in her voice, no censure or accusation or disappointment. Antonio found himself returning her smile, then taking Ella from her as he kissed Maisie hello with passion, warmth and gratitude.

She pressed one palm against his cheek as they rested their foreheads against one another's. 'I'm glad you're here,' she said softly.

'So am I.' And truly he was.

Ella started to squirm and Antonio stepped away, jiggling her in his arms, half amazed at how normal it had become to soothe his daughter. Maisie watched them both for a moment, a smile on her face, and then went to make dinner. Yes, this was normal. He had to remind himself that, make himself believe it. It was normal…and it was wonderful.

Dinner was relaxed but also a little bit chaotic, with them taking it in turns to hold and bounce Ella, who was restless. Antonio gave her a bath and then Maisie put her to bed, coming downstairs afterwards, a shy and expectant look on her face.

This part, Antonio knew, was simple, and yet just as wonderful as all that had gone before. Silently he took her by the hand and led her upstairs. Silently he closed her bedroom door and then drew her into his arms, kissing her softly and yet with increasing urgency, because he couldn't hold her in his arms and not want her.

She returned his kisses with just as much urgency and eagerness, her body pressed against his, her arms wrapped around him. Somehow they fell onto the bed in a tangle of limbs, and then they were shedding clothes as fast as they could, the urgency and need overwhelming them both.

Yet amidst the tidal wave of desire Antonio sought to anchor himself in the moment, in Maisie. Braced above her on his forearms, he gazed down at her lovely face, her golden-red curls spread across the white pillowcase in a fiery cloud.

I love you. The words rose in his throat and sat heavily in his mouth. Words so many people found easy to say, and yet he could not make himself say them. He wasn't sure he felt them and, if he did, he didn't want to. Love meant risk and fear and pain. Love meant anger and arguing and disappointment. He couldn't shake that deep-seated certainty, the leaden weight of it that had sat in his gut for far too many years. *I love you.*

He kissed her instead, trying to imbue some of what he felt—the good part, at least—in his kiss, in the gentle ferocity of it. And he thought, perhaps wrongly, that Maisie understood, for she kissed him back as she wrapped her legs around him and drew him into her body, accepting all of him, just as he was.

CHAPTER FIFTEEN

SPRING BLOSSOMED INTO SUMMER, the weeks sliding lazily by, as Maisie revelled in and clung to a happiness which felt both overwhelming and fragile. Antonio came over most days, either after work or sometimes taking the afternoon off. They spent simple hours with Ella, taking a walk or going on an excursion somewhere a bit further away, both of them finding happiness in simply being together.

They also went into Milan several times, for various engagements, and, while Maisie found she enjoyed those experiences of elegance and luxury with Antonio by her side, she was always glad to be back in her home. Their home.

Besides the mother-and-baby group she'd joined, she'd managed to pick up a few violin pupils through connections in the village and was now tutoring several times a week, while Ella napped.

The nights Antonio spent with Maisie were just as, if not more so, wonderful as the days. As they learned each other's bodies, the wonder of their first union deepened into something more profound and intimate, each act feeling to Maisie as if she was bound more and more closely to Antonio...or at least he was bound to her.

For the truth was, despite the time she'd spent with Antonio, in his company and in his bed, she still didn't trust how he felt, and she suspected he didn't either. She'd given herself several stern talking-tos about it, telling herself to be patient, to stay calm, and, while most of the time she managed this, on the days when he didn't visit, on the nights when she was alone, the old fears crept in.

Memories of her parents' sudden death, the way her life had felt like a chessboard swept clean, the carefully ordered pawns toppled by one careless moment, hounded and haunted her. She'd survived the tumult and grief, but only just. She didn't think she could survive it again. And she knew it would be worse if Antonio walked away from her. He wouldn't be taken in a senseless tragedy. He would choose it, and she would let him, and that felt awful. She'd found love, but she still didn't know how to be strong. How to fight for it.

In the middle of July, when Ella was five months old and the summer heat was scorching, Maisie told Max about her and Antonio. She'd kept it from him for a while because she hadn't wanted him to worry, especially not when he was so clearly enjoying life without the concerns of a sister and niece.

'You're *with* Rossi?' he asked on a video call, his eyebrows rising towards his hairline as Maisie sat in front of the computer screen, Ella in her lap.

'Yes, and please don't call him "Rossi", Max, as if he's some stranger.'

'But do you really know him, Maisie? He *was* a stranger—'

'And he isn't now.' Ella blew a raspberry at the screen and Maisie let out a somewhat shaky laugh. As confident as she wanted to feel about all this, Max's surprise was reminding her of how uncertain everything still felt. 'We've come to know each other over these last few months, Max,' she continued. 'Antonio is a good man and…and the truth is, I love him.' As soon as she'd said the words, she wished she could snatch them back. She hadn't said them before to anyone, and Antonio certainly hadn't said them to her. Sometimes Maisie felt as if he was making a point of *not* saying them.

'Oh, Maisie.' Max couldn't hide his concern, and that made Maisie feel worse.

'What? Is it wrong to love someone?'

'Not wrong, but maybe dangerous. Not that I'm one to talk. I've never been in love.' He gave a mock shudder, and Maisie tried to smile. 'I just don't want you to get hurt. You've had enough sadness in your life, Maise. We both have.'

'I know. I don't want any more sadness, trust me.'

'Do you really think Ros—Antonio can make you happy? Can settle down?'

Maisie tried for a laugh. 'Those are two different questions.'

'But they're definitely related.'

'True.' She sighed and set a squirming Ella on a fleecy blanket on the floor. Her daughter was doing her best to sit up by herself, giving Maisie beaming, drooling grins all the while. Maisie's heart clenched with love for her daughter.

'And what about Ella?' Max asked, making Maisie jerk up.

'What about her?'

'You don't want her to get hurt, either,' Max said seriously. 'If Antonio isn't in it for the long haul, Maisie…'

'Maybe he is.' Her heart had started thumping uncomfortably. She didn't like what Max was saying, but she couldn't really blame him for saying it. She knew he had her best interests at heart. He was only saying what she'd tried not to think about herself.

Max looked so sceptical that Maisie wished she could laugh, but she couldn't. It mattered too much. It hurt too deeply. 'Maisie,' her brother said. 'The man is a known playboy. One internet search was all I needed to do. Do you know how many women he's dated? Supermodels and actresses and all the rest? None of them has lasted more than a week, usually less. A lot less.'

'I know that.' Maisie's chest felt tight as she sought to keep her voice steady. 'I know his reputation, Max.' Even if she tried not to dwell on it.

'So why do you think he's changed?' Max's hazel eyes were full of compassion and, Maisie feared, pity. 'Why do you think he's different with you?'

What a question. How on earth could she answer it? Because it felt different? Because she *wanted* it to be different, so, so badly? 'I don't know,' she whispered. Her throat was starting to thicken and she blinked rapidly. 'He just is, Max. At least… I hope he is. With me.' Which said it all, really. Sometimes that felt like all she had…hope.

Max was silent for a long moment, and Maisie could hardly look at him. She'd had three of the happiest months of her life, and yet here she was, still in a welter of fear and uncertainty. But was that her fault…or Antonio's? They were both broken, scarred people, in different ways.

'I'm just worried for you, Maise,' Max said quietly. 'That's all. I want you to be happy. You know that, don't you?'

'Yes, of course I know that.' Maisie managed a watery smile. 'Thank you, Max.'

'You've done so much for me,' he persisted. 'And it's the least I can do to give you a bit of a warning. It might seem like tough love, but you gave me that over the years, didn't you?' His smile was wobbly and wry. 'Remember when I went to that party when I was seventeen and came back drunk?'

'I might,' Maisie said with a little answering smile. 'I held the bucket while you were sick into it.'

'Yeah.' Max's smile turned sheepish and apologetic. 'Sorry about that. But my point is, you grounded me for two weeks. I was annoyed and angry at the time, but I know now you were right to do it. You did the hard stuff because you loved me.'

'And this is you doing the hard stuff?' Maisie brushed at her eyes. 'Well, thanks. I do appreciate it, Max. I know you're looking out for me.'

'And you know if it all goes wrong or ends badly, you've got a home with me? No matter what?'

Maisie suppressed a shudder at the thought of it ending badly. 'Thank you,' she whispered. 'I mean that.'

After she'd said goodbye, Maisie buckled Ella into her stroller and went for a walk, mainly to clear her head of her endlessly circling thoughts and fears. After living there for three months, the narrow, winding streets had become familiar to her, as had the central square with its fountain and square for *bocce*. As she sat on a bench and watched the men bowl, the sun warm on her arms and face, she tried to let the worries die down.

So Antonio hadn't said he loved her yet. She knew he was trying, and she thought he was happy. It should be okay. Saying three little words wasn't insurance for anything, anyway. Her parents had told her they'd loved her plenty of times, and look how that had ended.

Sudden tears filled her eyes. Was she always going to be haunted by the ghosts of her past, the old hurts and griefs, just as Antonio was? She'd thought she'd healed, or at least as much as you could from losing people you loved, but loving Antonio showed her how afraid she still was. Not of him dying the way her parents had, necessarily, but of losing him all the same.

Ella was beginning to fuss and so, with a heavy heart, Maisie rose from the bench and started back towards the villa. She told herself she had so much to be thankful for—a beautiful home, a healthy baby, a kind and compassionate man in her life, new friends and, more recently, the opportunity to teach violin. She was really very blessed. Why couldn't she be happy with what she had? Why did she have to constantly worry about losing it, and all the while wanting more?

Her mobile trilled as she came into the house, and a glance at the screen told her it was Antonio.

'Where are you?' he asked as she unbuckled Ella from her stroller, the phone cradled between her neck and ear.

'I'm at home. Why?'

'I'm sending a car for you. I've got an engagement tonight and I need you there.'

'You do?' She hadn't been to a social event since that first charity gala, and now she found herself both excited and slightly annoyed by the possibility. 'Antonio, it's already four o'clock and Ella hasn't even been fed—'

'You can bring her as well. I'll hire a babysitter.'

Maisie took a deep breath, determined not to find fault unnecessarily. The truth was, it would be fun to go out, and Ella was taking bottles easily now. 'All right,' she said. 'I'll get her ready.'

Antonio paced the living area of the penthouse as Maisie got ready in his bedroom. They'd spent very little time together in his apartment; in fact, she hadn't been there since the night of the charity gala, when he'd felt as if his very soul were being blown apart and then reformed as something new and fragile. He had, Antonio reflected, compartmentalised his life quite neatly. Maisie and Ella tucked away in their villa, and his bachelor life in the city. Not that he'd taken advantage of the separation; he couldn't begin to imagine being with another woman when he had Maisie in his life. But he'd done it unconsciously, as a way to keep that little bit of distance that felt so necessary and that he knew, deep down, could be so destructive.

He wasn't immune to the flash of disappointment he saw in Maisie's eyes when he pulled away from her, or didn't stay the night, or didn't say the words he knew she was waiting to hear.

Tonight was, he hoped, a way to remedy that. He was trying, he wanted to try, and he hoped Maisie realised that, because it was all he had to give.

'I'm ready.'

He turned at the sound of her quiet voice, and then drew his breath in sharply at the lovely sight of her. Her evening gown was a column of royal blue, emphasising her lush, lithe figure perfectly, and making her hair, worn loose about her face and shoulders, look like a golden-red crown.

'You look like a queen.'

'And you look like a king.' She smiled uncertainly, and Antonio reached for her hand. Ella was already down for the night, the babysitter he'd engaged happy to listen for her. The evening was theirs.

'Come,' he said, and she did.

Antonio started to relax once they got to the engagement—a fundraising gala sponsored by one of his clients—and they began to circulate. Maisie, despite her nervousness, was a natural at chatting and socialising, her warmth and friendliness shining through. As ever, he was proud to have her on his arm—and he wanted her to know it. To feel it.

And even though he didn't have the words, he thought she did feel it; he felt it himself in the smiles she slid his way, the way her eyes lit up, sparkling jade.

'You were magnificent,' he told her when they were alone later, the babysitter dismissed, the apartment quiet and dark all around them. He drew her into his arms and she rested her head against his shoulder, both of them relaxed in the embrace.

'It seems so surreal,' Maisie said softly, her forehead pressed against his shoulder.

'What does?'

'Parties, limos, even the villa I live in.' She paused, took a breath. 'You.'

Antonio tensed. He'd been expecting this conversation, had known it would become necessary, but he still didn't welcome it. He didn't feel ready. 'Me?' he answered carefully. 'What do you mean?'

'I just...' Maisie let out a shuddering breath. 'I don't know what's real, Antonio. What to trust. What to believe.'

'Is it so very difficult?' He tried to keep his voice even. 'We've been happy, haven't we, Maisie, these last few months?'

'Happy...yes.' She lifted her head to gaze at him seriously. 'But happiness is fleeting, wonderful as it is, and I honestly don't know whether our happiness has any sure foundation.' She scanned his face, searching for an answer that Antonio didn't think she'd be able to find. 'Does it, Antonio?' she asked quietly. 'Are we...are we working towards something more? Something bigger than just this moment?'

His chest felt tight, a pressure growing that made it hard to speak. 'We're trying,' he said at last. 'Isn't that enough?'

'I thought it was. I want it to be. And sometimes it has been. But...' Maisie let out a soft, sad sigh. 'You still feel so distant to me sometimes. Almost as if you're intentionally cutting yourself off. And it makes me afraid, which might be my weakness, because I know what it is to lose somebody, and I don't want to again.'

'You won't lose me, Maisie,' Antonio said, his voice rough with emotion. 'Not that way.'

'But another way?' she persisted softly, and Antonio couldn't answer. So he kissed her instead, tenderly, thoroughly, and thankfully Maisie let herself be kissed.

CHAPTER SIXTEEN

'A DAY FOR ME?'

Maisie blinked at Antonio uncertainly, the whole idea entirely novel and unexpected. She was lying in bed, the sun streaming through the windows, while he stretched out next to her, a cat-like grin on his undeniably handsome face.

'Yes, for you. Why not? You work so hard, taking care of Ella, and you deserve to be pampered. I've arranged some beauty treatments and a full body massage for you at a local spa.' His grin turned teasingly wolfish as he added, 'Of course, I could give you the full body massage myself...'

'You could.' Maisie scooted up in bed, her mind still whirling. Last night she'd felt close to Antonio, despite the way the conversation had ended—with kisses rather than words. She told herself kisses could be enough, and today he seemed smiling and relaxed, which made her smiling and relaxed too. 'I can't remember the last time I've had a whole day to myself.'

'Exactly.'

'But Ella...'

'Can manage without you for the day. I'll take care of her, and I'll bring her back to the villa and put her to bed. It'll be good for me. For us.'

'Yes…' She shook her head slowly as she let out a laugh. 'I don't know what to say.'

'Say yes.'

'Okay.' Maisie grinned; suddenly it seemed easy. 'Thank you.'

Antonio pulled her close for a kiss. 'My pleasure.'

An hour later Antonio's driver dropped her off at a luxurious-looking spa, Ella asleep in her car seat next to Antonio in the back of the limo.

'I hope you'll manage,' Maisie said with a bit of a grimace. 'She's been grumpy for the last few days… I think she's coming down with a cold.'

'We'll be fine,' Antonio assured her. 'I think I can manage twelve hours or so, if only just.'

'Right.' She was fussing, but only because this would be the longest she'd been away from Ella since she'd been born. 'Thank you,' Maisie said, and with one last kiss she slipped out of the car.

Within minutes of stepping through the elegant tinted glass doors of the spa she was swept away by several glamorous assistants, and in only a few more minutes Maisie found herself in a dimly lit room with soothing music playing in the background, sipping a fruit smoothie as someone massaged her feet. She'd expected to feel awkward and nervous, but what she felt was sheer bliss.

She couldn't remember when she'd last been able to properly relax, to let herself be pampered. She leaned her head back against the seat and closed her eyes.

The day flew by in a whirlwind of treatments—manicure, pedicure, massage, facial, haircut. As Maisie sat in a deep armchair waiting for her toenails to dry, one of the staff handed her a stack of magazines to look at and a foaming cappuccino sprinkled with chocolate. Bliss.

She'd checked in with Antonio a few hours ago, and

he'd assured her that all was fine. Now she flipped open the gossip magazine and happily immersed herself in the fairy-tale world of celebrities.

By the time the day of treatments was finished, Maisie was glowing on the outside but feeling restless and a little bit anxious to see both Antonio and Ella again. She wanted their arms around her, to revel in the warm embrace of her daughter and the man she loved.

Antonio had arranged for a car to fetch her and take her back to the villa, and she slid into its sumptuous interior with a breath of relief, happiness buoying inside her at the thought of seeing them both soon.

When she arrived back at the villa, however, the house was empty and dark. Her joyous expectation soured to unease. It was nearly seven o'clock, Ella's bedtime. Why on earth was Antonio out, and where was he? The stroller was in the front hall, so he hadn't taken Ella for a walk. Where could he have gone?

Maisie combed through the entire house and garden while she rang Antonio's mobile over and over, only to have it switch to voicemail every time. Where was he? Where was her daughter? Unease gave way to panic as unlikely yet terrifying scenarios ran through her head, fuelled by the uncertainty that was always seething under the surface, waiting to strike.

Had Antonio just *left*? Left her? Had he taken Ella somewhere, decided he'd had enough? Maybe the spa day had been some sort of awful ruse.

Maisie told herself she was being ridiculously paranoid. She knew she was, that no matter how remote Antonio had seemed sometimes, she had no reason to distrust him that much. She loved him, and she hoped in time he would love her.

And yet. *And yet*.

Once before the playing field of her life had been torn up. Once before everything she'd thought certain had been swept away in a single moment. It was hard, so hard, not to fear it happening again. Not to brace herself for it, because that was what life did. It turned on you, pulled the rug right out from under you and left you flat on your back, reeling and devastated.

Twenty minutes after she'd returned to the darkened house Antonio finally rang. Maisie answered with a gasp of relief.

'Where are you?' she demanded before either of them had had a chance to say hello. 'Where have you been?'

'Maisie—' Antonio's voice broke and Maisie went cold.

'What's happened?' she asked numbly. 'What's wrong?'

'It's Ella,' Antonio said, and Maisie's legs turned weak as she swayed where she stood.

'No,' she whispered. 'No, please.'

'We're at the hospital. I didn't have time to send a car, or ring you, or anything…'

'What's happened?' Her voice rose on a cry of pure terror. 'Antonio, what's happened to my baby?'

'They're saying it's meningitis.'

Maisie let out a soft cry. Meningitis. A parent's worst nightmare, for the disease moved so quickly and aggressively.

'Are you at home?'

'Yes.' Maisie gulped back a useless sob. 'But I'll come now. Just tell me which hospital and I'll come right away.'

Maisie knew she was in no fit state to drive. Twenty minutes later the taxi she'd called pulled into the paediatric unit of the nearest hospital, Maisie's heart thudding harder than ever. Antonio met her at the doors, ushering her quickly inside.

'How is she? How did this happen?'

'She's stable at the moment—'

'At the moment?' Panic clawed at Maisie's insides. She couldn't lose Ella. She just couldn't. 'What does that mean?'

'She has bacterial meningitis,' Antonio said quietly. His voice was steady but his face was taut and pale, his eyes like dark shadows. 'At least they think she does. It came on so suddenly…' His voice choked and he took a quick breath. 'I thought she was just upset because of a cold or teething…'

'Just let me see her.' Maisie couldn't bear to hear any more, not when she hadn't even seen Ella. 'Where is she?'

Moments later Maisie stood in front of a bassinet, Ella's inert body lying in it, tubes snaking out of her. She looked tiny and so very sick. Tears started in her eyes and she brushed them away angrily, too impatient, too anxious to give in to such emotion now.

'What are they saying, Antonio? What's the prognosis?'

'They don't know.'

'So she might…she might…'

'We just have to wait and see, Maisie. She's got the antibiotics she needs, and it's just a matter of time to see how she responds, if there's been any damage.' An internet search on her phone had informed her of the potential dangers. Brain damage, deafness, death. Maisie closed her eyes.

'How could you let this happen?' The question was squeezed out of her, a desperate whisper of the utmost pain. 'I was gone one day. *One day* I left her, and now this.' She shook her head, wrapping her arms around herself, and turned away from him, filled with grief and fear.

'How could you let this happen?'

The question echoed through the emptiness inside him, reverberating on and on. He'd heard it before, when his mother had heard that Paolo was dead. She'd turned her anguished eyes on Antonio and demanded to know how, and he'd had no answer. No excuse. It was the same now, and to his shame Antonio saw the same anguish and accusation in Maisie's eyes that he'd seen in his mother's.

'How could you let this happen?'

How could he? The one day he'd had sole charge of his daughter, he'd risked her life. Unknowingly, perhaps, but it had been the same with Paolo. His actions, or lack of them, were the direct cause of Ella's situation. If he'd taken her to the doctor sooner, if he'd considered the signs and symptoms, if he'd acted faster… Instead he'd waited far too long, thinking that Ella had nothing more than a cold. He'd been stupidly lulled into a false sense of security. So stupidly.

He'd thought he was being careful, keeping his distance, but he'd only been protecting himself, not the person—the people—he loved most. He hated himself for it. His selfishness was unforgivable.

'She hasn't had the vaccine,' Maisie said in a leaden voice. 'They don't offer it in America until children are older, but I should have thought…going to another country, I should have thought…'

'It's not your fault,' Antonio answered in a low voice. 'It's mine. I… I waited too long.'

'How long did you wait?' Maisie turned to him, her eyes wide and frantic, and Antonio bowed his head under her rightful judgement.

'I put her down for a nap and when several hours had passed I went to check on her. She was unresponsive, floppy… I called an ambulance right away, but they took so long to arrive…'

'Hours, then.' Maisie hugged herself, as if she was cold, despite the warm air. 'All it takes is hours.'

'I know.' He'd learned far more about meningitis than he'd ever wanted to know as he'd waited for Ella to start to respond to the antibiotics. 'I know. It's all my fault.' Maisie didn't reply, and that was all the answer he needed.

Once again he'd endangered the life of someone he loved deeply and dearly. Only time would tell whether this would be as devastating and fatal as Paolo's accident had been.

The hours ticked by, endless and agonising, as Maisie and Antonio waited for news, isolated in their private worlds of grief and fear. Antonio didn't, in his own wretched guilt, attempt to comfort Maisie, or offer her false words of hope. It surely was not his place, and in any case Maisie barely looked at him. She wanted nothing from him now, and he couldn't blame her.

Then, finally, in the pearly light of dawn, with both of them nursing cold cups of coffee in a stupor of fatigue and fear, news came.

'Ella is beginning to respond to the antibiotics.' The doctor spoke in Italian and Maisie glanced wildly between him and Antonio, her frantic expression demanding an immediate translation. He gave it to her, and she sagged with relief, tears finally, after a long, dry night, springing to her eyes.

'Thank God,' she whispered. 'Thank God.'

Antonio asked the doctor a few more questions, and he answered in Italian again, while Maisie waited impatiently. After the doctor had left, Antonio steered her towards a quiet alcove.

'What is it, Antonio?' she demanded. 'Is there something bad you're not telling me?'

'I'll tell you everything.' And he did, explaining what the doctor had said, how it would still be another twenty-four to forty-eight hours before they knew whether Ella had suffered any lasting effects from the bacterial infection. But at least she was going to survive.

Maisie's shoulders sagged with relief. She looked as if she could collapse where she stood.

'You need to sleep,' Antonio told her.

'I won't leave the hospital,' she warned him fiercely.

He held both his hands up in supplication. 'Of course not. There is a room for parents of ill children. I'll come and get you if there's any news or anything changes.'

'What will you do?'

'I'll stay and wait.'

'Then I should too—'

'Maisie.' Antonio kept his voice gentle, his throat aching. 'Ella is going to need you more than ever in the next days and weeks. Rest while you can. I swear to you on my life, I will come and get you if you're needed, or if she so much as stirs.'

Maisie stared at him for a long moment, weighing up his words, whether to believe him. Then slowly she nodded.

'Thank you,' she said, and Antonio gave her directions to the room where she could rest. As she walked away he felt his heart, that stony object that he'd thought he'd been keeping separate and safe, begin to shatter.

CHAPTER SEVENTEEN

MAISIE HADN'T EXPECTED to be able to fall asleep, but mere moments after curling up on the pull-out sofa in the parents' waiting room she fell into a deep, dreamless slumber. Hours later she startled awake, feeling utterly wretched, her eyelids glued together, her mouth dry, her hair wild, her heart thudding.

She scrambled for her phone and checked the time. Antonio hadn't come. As quickly as she could, Maisie jammed her feet into her shoes and combed her fingers through her hair before wrenching open the door and hurrying into the hallway.

She found Antonio sitting in an armchair next to Ella's cot, his face unshaven, his hair mussed, his gaze steady on their daughter, making Maisie wonder if he'd so much as blinked the whole time he'd been waiting there, keeping vigil.

'Antonio.' She spoke softly as she came into the room, and he turned to glance at her, his expression turning guarded.

'The consultant just came in. She thinks Ella is making some improvement.'

'That's great.' Relief poured through her in a sweet rush.

'I was going to get you,' Antonio said. 'I swear.'

'I believe you.' She gazed at him uncertainly through

the haze of both physical and emotional exhaustion. There was something different about him, something other than the fatigue and fear she knew they were both feeling. He seemed...resigned, although Ella was going to get better.

'You should get some sleep,' she said.

'No.' He shook his head. 'I'm fine.' But he didn't look fine. His eyes were dark hollows, his face seeming thinner and more gaunt under a day's worth of stubble. And his manner was frighteningly remote.

'A coffee, then,' Maisie said, feeling a sudden, sweet need to take care of him, to offer what comfort she could. For the last twelve hours she'd been in an isolated bubble of her own terror, but she wanted to reach out now. She wanted to lean on Antonio, and let him lean on her. But it appeared he didn't want that because he rose from the chair stiffly and walked to the window, his back to her.

'Why don't you sit with her?' he suggested. 'The consultant will come back soon.'

The next few hours passed in a strained blur of waiting. Antonio barely spoke to her, and Maisie grappled with what to say to him, how to reach him when he seemed more remote than he'd ever been.

Then Ella woke up, bringing them both to the brink of tears, and Maisie held her for a short while, savouring the soft feel of her tiny limbs, the baby powder and milk smell of her now mingled with the bitter tang of antibiotics and the antiseptic smell of the hospital.

In the late afternoon the consultant told them the worst was over. Ella would be able to go home the following day, hopefully without any lasting ill-effects, although they'd need to bring her back in a week for another check. Maisie could hardly believe they'd all emerged intact from the wreckage of the last twenty-four hours. She'd felt as if she'd lived an entire lifetime in the space of a single day, and she was a changed person.

That night Maisie settled Ella in her cot, thrilling to her daughter's sleepy smile, before she and Antonio returned to the waiting room. She hadn't showered in what felt like an age, and the spa treatments of yesterday seemed like a dream. 'You should go home and get some sleep,' he said. 'I'll stay here.'

'Antonio, you must be exhausted—'

'I'm fine.'

Maisie was reluctant to leave her daughter for even a second, but Antonio was resolute and she recognised that she needed to be rested and well for when Ella came home in the morning.

'All right,' she relented.

'You can take your car,' he added. 'It's parked in the garage.'

Surprise made her stiffen. 'The car...but who drove it?' She knew that Antonio hadn't been behind the wheel since the day his brother had died.

'I did,' Antonio said starkly. 'The ambulance was too long coming, so I put Ella in her car seat and drove her to the hospital.'

A lump formed in Maisie's throat. She could not imagine how hard that must have been for him, to face his worst fear all over again, and for their daughter's sake. 'Oh, Antonio...' She laid a hand on his arm, and he went still, not looking at her.

Maisie gazed at him with growing dread, a leaden fear weighing down her insides. She hadn't been imagining the strain and distance that had appeared between them in the last day. She just didn't know why it had happened, or what it meant. 'Thank you,' she whispered. Antonio didn't answer. He didn't even look at her, and after a few awful seconds Maisie removed her hand from his arm.

When they were back home, she told herself, things would return to normal between them. They'd be a family again, stronger than ever, brought together by this near-tragedy. She told herself that, over and over, but she couldn't make herself believe it.

After a night that held less sleep than she would have liked, she returned to the hospital, thankful to be holding Ella once again. Though still sleepy and weak, Ella seemed much more the happy baby she usually was, eager to be held and cuddled.

Antonio didn't speak all the way back to the villa, and Maisie kept her attention on Ella, afraid of what she'd see in his face. Nothing good, she suspected, although she was afraid to think of what or why.

She found out soon enough, when they'd returned to the villa and she'd settled Ella down for a nap. Maisie came downstairs to find Antonio standing by the door, the flat look in his eyes chilling her.

'I think it's better if we go back to the way things were,' he said, his tone cold and final.

Maisie's mouth went bone-dry, her head spinning. 'The way things were?'

'I'll visit three times a week and have Ella on Saturdays, if that's agreeable to you?'

'You mean…' She wasn't surprised, and yet at the same time she was devastated. 'You mean you're…you're breaking up with me?' Silly, teenaged words for what felt like such a monumental event, an earthquake destroying all her hopes and desires.

'It can't work, Maisie. That much is clear.'

'But…why?'

He just shook his head.

'Antonio…' Maisie struggled for the right words to reach him. 'Why are you doing this?' she asked brokenly, because she didn't have anything else.

'I tried.' It sounded so awful, so bleak. 'I tried, and I failed. I'm sorry.'

'You didn't fail—'

'I did. And I can't face that, Maisie. I can't risk it again.'

'But—'

'It's better this way.'

Maisie stared at him helplessly, longing to break through the stony barricade he'd surrounded himself with. Wanting to fight for her, for him, for them, and yet Antonio seemed so unreachable. 'Antonio…' she tried, not knowing what words would bring him back to her.

'I'll see you the day after tomorrow.' He paused. 'Of course, if you need more childcare help, just say the word. I can arrange a part-time nanny—'

'I don't want a nanny,' Maisie spat. Suddenly she was furious. How dared he give up on them so easily? 'I want you. Antonio, why are you doing this?'

Antonio stared at Maisie, her vivid eyes and stricken face, and he squared both his shoulders and his jaw. This was hard, but staying together would be harder. Would bring more chance of heartache, of disappointment, of tragedy. He saw that now. He saw it so very clearly, and he couldn't cope with failing again. Losing again.

'I told you, it's better this way. Better for you, Maisie.' He heard the throb of sincerity as well as regret in his voice, and thought she did too. 'I can't make you happy. I wish I could, but I can't.'

'Isn't that for me to decide?'

'When would you decide it?' Antonio demanded, pain ripping through him, spilling through the seams. 'In a

week? A month? A year? When you'd had your heart broken, or, God forbid, when Ella—?' He couldn't go on.
Something in him was breaking, splitting right open, and
he couldn't bear it.

He wrenched open the door and started walking blindly
towards the waiting car. Blood pounded in his ears and his
heart thudded; he felt dizzy with the enormity of what he
was doing, the pain of it all. He thought this would hurt
less, but right now it didn't feel like it. He couldn't imagine anything hurting more.

He slid inside the car and rested his head against the
back seat. The driver hesitated, and Antonio forced himself to speak.

'Drive on, please.'

'But...'

A fist pounded on the window, making his eyes fly open.
Maisie stood there, looking wild, her eyes glittering, her
face flushed, her hair a Titian nimbus about her face. Antonio stared at her dumbly, too shocked to move. Then she
pulled open the door with a vicious yank.

'Don't you dare walk out on me,' she said, her voice low
and savage. 'Don't you dare play the martyr when you're
really a coward.'

'What—?'

'Yes, Antonio, a coward.' Her voice broke and tears
sparkled in her eyes. 'You're going to walk out on me, on
my daughter, on us as a couple and a family, and for what
earthly reason?'

'I told you—'

'Because you're scared,' she finished furiously, tears
streaking down her cheeks. 'Because loving someone is
scary and it hurts and you risk so much. Do you think I
don't know that? That I haven't experienced it as much as
you have? For the whole time I've been with you, I've let

you call the shots. I've been too weak to do anything but let you play the tune. But not this time, Antonio. Not when so much is on the line.'

She was furious and beautiful, the most glorious thing he'd ever seen. Still he persisted. 'Maisie—'

'*No*. You listen to me now, Antonio. We almost lost our daughter yesterday and it would have been the worst thing that had ever happened to either of us, which is saying something considering what we've both already been through. But it should bring us together, Antonio, not pull us apart.'

'Maybe it showed us what we're really made of.'

She stared at him hard, her tear-filled eyes narrowing. 'Then what are you made of, Antonio?'

She wanted to hear the ugly truth? Fine. He'd give it to her. Maybe he was a coward, because he'd kept it from her in the first place, but he'd tell it to her now. In one swift, fluid movement Antonio got out of the car, ordering the driver to wait. He strode back into the house and Maisie followed, closing the door behind her and then folding her arms.

'Well?' she asked quietly, composed now. 'Tell me what you meant.'

'I can't do this,' Antonio said in a low voice. 'I can't be enough for you or Ella. I can't be responsible...'

'Responsible for what, Antonio?'

'I can't make another mistake,' he ground out. 'Like I did with Paolo. I can't risk that, not for your sake, or Ella's, or my own.'

She stared at him, her eyes narrowed, her mouth compressed. 'So what's the alternative? Never letting anyone in? Never loving anyone, ever?'

He looked away, unable to meet her gaze. 'If that's the only choice.'

Maisie was silent for a long moment. 'You blame yourself for this,' she said at last, the words coming out slowly as realisation crept over her face. 'You blame yourself. Why, Antonio—?'

'You said it as well,' he couldn't keep from answering. 'You asked me why I let this happen.'

Her mouth opened and then closed. Her eyes widened. Finally, stricken, she whispered, 'You think I blame *you*...?'

'As I blame myself. If I'd noticed the symptoms earlier, if I'd checked on her while she was napping... What if she'd died, Maisie?' He heard how ragged his voice had become, how desperate as the remembered pain and fear lashed through him again, a lash he knew he would feel repeatedly. 'What if she'd died? It would have been my fault.'

'But she didn't die, Antonio.'

'Even so...'

'Why are you so hard on yourself?' she demanded, her voice as pain-filled as his. 'Yes, I said that, but it was in a moment of terror and I didn't mean it. I don't blame you, I swear. You drove her to the hospital yourself, and I know how much that cost you. Antonio, I admire you, I respect you. I—' Her voice hitched. 'I love you,' she whispered. 'I've loved you for months now, and I know you don't love me, but...'

He couldn't let her words pass, even though he knew he was hurting them both. It wasn't fair for her not to know, to think her feelings weren't returned when they were, a hundredfold. 'I do love you,' he said in a low voice. 'I have for a while, even if I've been deceiving myself. And that's why I'm doing this. To spare you—'

'You call this sparing me?' she cut across him, her voice rising. 'Antonio, love means pain. It means getting hurt, and it also means forgiveness. I know you still suffer from what happened with your brother, and if your parents still blame you in some way, that is on them, not on you.' Her voice turned as fierce as her expression as she crossed the room and grabbed him by the shoulders. 'Love forgives. Love doesn't remember wrongs. Love never fails.' She shook him gently. 'Do you believe that? Because if we love each other, then we can move past this. If we love each other, we can move past any hurt or wrong, because we *forgive*. Even if you were to blame. Even if I'd messed up. Even if Ella had died. That's what love does, Antonio. That's what it is. I've lost everything before and I can't bear to again. That's what kept me being afraid with you, but I don't want to be afraid now. I want to be brave, for you, for me, for *us*. Don't let this one thing sink us, not when we have so much to live for. To love for. *Please*.'

While he stared at her, shocked, his mind reeling from the truth and power of her words, Maisie stood up on her tiptoes and, wrapping her arms around him, brushed a kiss across his lips.

'I love you,' she whispered against his mouth. 'I love you so much, and you've said you love me. There's no reason on earth to walk away from what we have together. No sin or mistake or anything can separate us.' She leaned back, scanning his face, the fierce light still brightening her eyes. 'Tell me, do you believe that?'

Antonio gazed into his beloved's face and knew only one answer could be given. The truth, which he'd been blinded to for so long. The truth that was the only thing that could set him free. 'Yes,' he said. 'I do.'

He took Maisie into his arms, burying his face in her fragrant hair as his body finally relaxed, his soul finally spilling out its pain and guilt. 'How did you become so wise?' he murmured against her hair, and she let out a shaky little laugh.

'By loving you. By realising, over these last few months,

what love is, and what it means to be strong. You've shown me, Antonio, in so many wonderful ways.' She leaned back to press her palm against his cheek. 'And the fact that you do love me…'

'I do, so very much. I should have said it long before now.' Recrimination made him grimace, but then Maisie shook her head.

'No more regret. No more guilt, please, for both our sakes. We're free. Love has set us free.'

'Yes, free,' Antonio agreed. He'd been imprisoned for so long, but the bars had been of his own foolish making. 'I'm free to love you and love Ella, which is all I want to do.' He smiled and kissed her tenderly. 'Thank you for being patient with me. For not letting me walk away.'

'I could never have done that,' Maisie admitted. 'Forget pride or self-respect or anything else. I need you, Antonio. I need you in my life, and so does Ella.'

'And I promise, I'll never leave. Never.'

A small smile curved Maisie's mouth and lit her eyes. 'Then this is our happily-ever-after,' she said teasingly as Antonio drew her into his arms and sealed it with a kiss.

EPILOGUE

MAISIE GAZED IN the mirror at her reflection, feeling both incredulous and happy. It was two years since she'd first met Antonio, and it was their wedding day. Max had flown over for the occasion, a quiet yet joyful ceremony in the small village church. Later there would be a reception in Milan for all of Antonio's business acquaintances and colleagues, but they'd wanted this ceremony to be just for family.

And there was more family than Maisie could have ever hoped for... Max and Ella, and, wonderfully, Antonio's parents. After hearing about Ella, they had reached out to him and begun to be reconciled with their son. Her heart was full.

Max knocked on the door and then poked his head in. 'My sister, the beautiful bride. Are you ready? Everyone is waiting.'

'Yes.' Maisie twitched her veil, glancing once more at the simple dress of broderie-anglaise that she'd chosen for her wedding gown.

'You look wonderful, Maisie.' Max reached for her hand. 'I'm so proud of you, and happy for you.'

'I'm happy for me,' Maisie said with a laugh. The last few months had been amazing, as she and Antonio had grown closer together. They'd purchased a larger family

home on the outskirts of Milan, and Maisie couldn't wait
to begin their life there together.

Taking Max's hand, she left the sacristy of the church
and paused on the threshold of the sanctuary, her heart
overflowing with love and thankfulness and joy. Antonio turned slightly, his eyes flaring with love and desire
as he caught sight of her. A small smile quirked his lips,
and Maisie grinned back with all the joy she felt. Then, her
head held high, she started down the aisle.

* * * * *

MILLS & BOON

Coming next month

THE SICILIAN'S BOUGHT CINDERELLA
Michelle Smart

'But...' Aislin couldn't form anything more than that one syllable. Dante's offer had thrown her completely.

His smile was rueful. 'My offer is simple, dolcezza. You come to the wedding with me and I give you a million euros.'

He pronounced it 'seemple', a quirk she would have found endearing if her brain hadn't frozen into a stunned snowball.

'You want to pay me to come to a wedding with you?'

'Si.' He unfolded his arms and spread his hands. 'The money will be yours. You can give as much or as little of it to your sister.'

It took a huge amount of effort to keep her voice steady. 'But you must have a heap of women you could take and not have to pay them for it.'

'None of them are suitable.'

'What does that mean?'

'I need to make an impression on someone and having you on my arm will assist in that.'

'A million dollars for one afternoon...?'

'I never said it would be for an afternoon. The celebrations will take place over the coming weekend.'

She tugged at her ponytail. 'Weekend?'

'Aislin, the groom is one of Sicily's richest men. It is a necessity that his wedding be the biggest and flashiest it can be.'

She almost laughed at the deadpan way he explained it.

She didn't need to ask who the richest man in Sicily was.

'If I'm going to accept your offer, what else do I need to know?'

'Nothing… Apart from that I will be introducing you as my fiancée.'

'What?' Aislin winced at the squeakiness of her tone.

'I require you to play the role of my fiancée.' His grin was wide with just a touch of ruefulness. The deadened, shocked look that had rung from his eyes only a few minutes before had gone. Now they sparkled with life and the effect was almost hypnotising.

She blinked the effect away.

'Why do you need a fiancée?'

'Because the father of the bride thinks going into business with me will damage his reputation.'

'How?'

'I will go through the reasons once I have your agreement on the matter. I appreciate it is a lot to take in so I'm going to leave you to sleep on it. You can give me your answer in the morning. If you're in agreement then I shall take you home with me and give you more details. We will have a few days to get to know each other and work on putting on a convincing act.'

'And if I say no?'

He shrugged. 'If you say no, then no million euros.'

Continue reading
THE SICILIAN'S BOUGHT CINDERELLA
Michelle Smart

Available next month
www.millsandboon.co.uk

COMING SOON!

We really hope you enjoyed reading this book. If you're looking for more romance, be sure to head to the shops when new books are available on

Thursday 24th January

To see which titles are coming soon, please visit
millsandboon.co.uk/nextmonth

LET'S TALK
Romance

For exclusive extracts, competitions and special offers, find us online:

- facebook.com/millsandboon
- @MillsandBoon
- @MillsandBoonUK

Get in touch on 01413 063232

For all the latest titles coming soon, visit
millsandboon.co.uk/nextmonth